Mara's Scrapbook

By

Carol Huebner

ISBN: 1-4033-0374-6 (Ebook)
ISBN: 1-4033-0375-4 (Softcover)

This book is printed on acid free paper.

1stBooks - rev. 5/7/02

Dedication

To honor Hazel, Mrs. D., Pauline and all strong women.

Preface

Mara sat in the dark. At first her back was stiff against the chair, but when she began to cry, her shoulders slumped over the table. She didn't say anything, didn't wail words into the darkness. In her mind was the sense that this diagnosis could be ignored, spontaneously float off to become a bad memory. But her mind was still rational enough not to form these ideas into spoken words. Instead, she pounded her fist on the table, over and over, and cried.

Finally, palms flattened against her forehead, she stared through the window. The moon was only a sliver, but city lights cast a glow, which lit the sky, and nearby hills, revealing their curves and shadowed grasses, and Mara stared at these. The view wasn't calming. Sounds of her children playing in the den, of her husband practicing the clarinet in his studio, didn't restore a sense of the routine.

No one was available to comfort her. She thought of Grandma Hazel, with her common sense, or Mrs. D., putting a fine touch on anything, but they were both long dead. In a while, she could certainly call Pauline, letting the sometimes-quivering voice wrap around her shoulders like a reassuring embrace.

But not now. Mara didn't reach for the lights. For the moment, darkness suited her.

I

Hazel Severn

Carol Huebner

Chapter 1

"Oatmeal," Hazel mumbled, balancing notepaper on the arm of the sofa. Immediately, she crossed off the word. Al had said that children don't like hot cereal, she thought. We grandparents may eat it every morning, never tire of it, but a six year old wants—what?

Frowning, Hazel poked at bits of yarn which stuck from the afghan draped across her lap. She was trying to remember magazine ads. What a thing to do, she thought, actually try to bring to mind those pictures, those ridiculous product names. Except suddenly, there it was, a grinning tiger above the name of a corn flake. Hazel wrote quickly. And I'd better buy some bowls in bright colors, she thought. What color had Phillip liked?

But it was impossible to remember her own son at six, and, letting her glasses drop on their chain, Hazel leaned her head against the back of the couch, eyelids closing gradually. Orange light from the fireplace mixed with gold from the lampshade above her pale skin, as she pictured her granddaughter's last visit.

Hazel could see Mara as a toddler, sitting on a booster seat at the kitchen table, not touching the hotdog, shaking her head at the mustard and ketchup Hazel had carefully set out in small glass dishes. On the one evening she'd stayed overnight, Hazel thought, Mara hadn't been the type to climb into my lap, hug me, beg for a story. Which I can understand. I sympathize with being a little withdrawn.

Hazel saw herself standing behind, then floating above, three aproned women in her own backyard. All the women looked like Betty Crocker, smiling as they unfolded a table and covered it with a paper cloth. After carefully smoothing the creases, they each hugged the Mara-child, then unwrapped first a plate of celery stalks filled with peanut butter, then a bowl of tiny gelatin animals surrounded by strawberry Jell-O, finally a platter of fried chicken with the skin pulled off and the meat loosened from the bone. The Mara-child clapped her tiny hands, eyes large with delight as she looked from each smiling face above the apron to the dish being offered for her enjoyment.

From behind them, Al's arm extended a white bowl steaming with oatmeal. The aproned women were motionless.

"You'll really like this, Petootie," he said to the child, who was frowning as she stared at the bowl. "Grandma added some honey and sprinkled on a few raisins. Hmm!"

"No!" Hazel cried, reaching out from behind the aprons, trying to grab the bowl. "I can do better, Mara!"

Al looked confused, and then with his free hand he swatted dark shapes hovering near the honey.

"Get away!" he scolded. "Shoo! Hazel, what is this? We don't usually have trouble with bees out here."

Buzz bzzzz.

Hazel jerked awake. The kitchen doorbell! Pushing aside the afghan and the magazines, she stood, wobbled for a moment, then walked quickly toward the kitchen. The shadow of a form peering in the window was blanketed by light as she flicked on the switch.

"Who is it?" she called, stooping over the door handle.

A man's voice answered, "Only me!" and Hazel turned the bolt.

"What in the world are you doing in the back yard?" she asked the tall man who stooped slightly as he entered, his white crew cut barely missing the molding.

"I was sticking in a campaign sign," the man explained as he shrugged out of his jacket.

"In the back yard? We've got one out front, Al."

"Back, front, wherever the neighbors can see it," Al laughed. Together they walked toward the hall closet, then the living room. Hazel resumed her place on the sofa, poking a strand of gray hair into her bun, tidying the sweater buttoned over her blouse. She was glad for Al's company.

"We got a fair amount done tonight," Al said over his shoulder as he poked the log. "A bunch of signs, some precinct calls. Of course," he added as he sank into the wing chair, "I would have gotten even more done if Rose hadn't shown up. That woman can't work without chatting."

"And she can't work *while* chatting," Hazel said, shaking her head. I can say that, she thought, even about my friend, because I'd say it to her face and she knows it.

"Oh well," Al said, arching his back in a stretch, "the election's Tuesday, so how much more can we do?"

Tuesday, Hazel thought. Amazing, how fast the months have gone by. It seems like only yesterday that Al and I were asked to clean up the office rented as a headquarters.

"You're so experienced," the campaign manager had assured them. "You know exactly what we need to make this place presentable. And of course," he'd said with a flourish toward his back pocket, "we'll reimburse you."

As if the money made me hesitate, she thought. That arrogant young fellow deserved my tongue-lashing! The idea that all we're good for is to get things ready for the *real* workers.

"I push a mean mop," Al had told her later, trying to calm her, "and there's no one faster with a toilet brush than you."

Suddenly back in the present, Hazel grabbed the paper still lying on the arm of the sofa and added to her list.

"Toilet brush," she said aloud.

"What?"

"I almost forgot. I need a new one."

Al waited until she had finished writing.

"Everyone asked about you. Did you get a lot of baking done?"

"Some," she answered. "A coffee cake, a couple dozen cookies."

"Good for you."

"But that's not enough, Al. I've been trying to think of things we should have around, but ideas just won't come."

Al laughed, a rolling, easy sound Hazel envied.

"Ideas not coming to *you*? That's a rarity! How about asking Rose? She sees her grandchildren pretty often. She'd know what kids like."

Hazel thought about that. Why had she felt reluctant when Rose, flushed and eager, had tried to pull her into a toy store? Because I'm not a grandma, she realized. It doesn't come naturally. And I can't entertain three people for a week, especially not *those* people: a son who's grown into somebody I don't much like, a daughter-in-law who's too ladylike, and a granddaughter we've hardly ever seen. Will Mara be glad she came or glad she never visits?

"You know what?" Hazel turned toward Al. "I guess I don't want them here."

Al squeezed her hand.

"Shy little thing," he teased, but Hazel pulled her hand away.

"This is serious, Al," she said. "I hadn't thought I'd be learning things about myself at this age, but there it is."

Al shrugged.

"Maybe you and I have gotten set in our ways" he suggested.

"Well, now," Hazel said. Maybe we have, she thought, smoothing the afghan against her lap. But I like our ways and I'm not crazy about interrupting them.

"Six letter word for honesty," she said quietly.

"Candor," Al answered promptly, and they were silent as they watched the fire.

Al let the door slam behind him.

"Yoohoo!" he called.

"In the kitchen," Hazel answered.

"Look!" he cried, holding out a newspaper as he came through the swinging door. "Dade won! The final count's in and he'll be our congressman!"

Hazel took the paper, raised her glasses and looked closely at the picture of Dade's smiling face.

"Where was this taken?"

Al poured himself a mug of coffee.

"Must have been some election party. Isn't that Rose next to him?"

Together they studied the photograph.

"Well," Hazel said, folding the paper and tossing it on the table, "I'm glad."

Al laughed.

"For Dade or for Rose?"

"For his constituents," Hazel answered. "I have strong feelings about representing the people well, and I think he'll do it."

Al put an arm around her shoulder.

"Selfless, that's what you are," he said.

Hazel leaned into his chest for a moment, then righted herself quickly.

"Not me," she mumbled. "I'm glad to have *you* around, aren't I?"

Good heavens, she thought, but Al didn't laugh.

"And I'm glad to be here," he said solemnly. "I wouldn't miss it for the world."

Hazel walked toward the shelf of cookbooks. I should make a fancy dinner, sort of a celebration, she thought, because of the election. And because of us.

Scrapbook, page 1

The cover is a deep red leather, scratched, showing the wear of years. Across the front is lettered SCRAPBOOK in gold script. The thick paper inside is a faded black, the first page flecked with dried bits of tape and triangular photo corners. Something was once there, in that place. A picture, an old letter. Over the years, something must have fallen out.

But in the corner, still stuck to the paper, is a black and white photograph of a young couple, she in large brimmed hat with a tight lace bodice and wide ribbon sash, he in stiff hat and collar with a bowtie. He has one hand around her waist, the other at the jacket slung over his shoulder, and a wedding band is visible, plain and narrow but shiny, as though new.

They are both smiling. His is actually more of a grin, almost triumphant, while hers is dainty, careful. She looks like a young lady, but something in her posture or her face says that she likes his hand touching her, she likes his grin, she enjoys having the photographer see them together. Perhaps she has waited a long time to be his wife, controlling her annoyance when other girls flirted with him, defending his high spirits when her parents tried to dissuade her. Perhaps she has been patient and now she is here as his wife, not just his girl.

Behind them in the picture are a ferris wheel and many people, milling around booths or rides, and small dogs sniffing the ground, but no one looks toward the couple. Surrounded by crowds, they stand separate, excited, confident about their day at the Fair.

Below their picture Mara has written in white, "GRANDMA AND GRANDPA, CHICAGO? CIRCA 1926." That is close enough.

Chapter 2

Hazel had always fought hard to keep her position, first as Al's favorite girl and fiancée, then as his wife who worked by his side at the upholstery store, advising customers about fabric and pattern, later as the mother of his son, and now as part of a retired couple. She had always felt that marriage to Al was something to be defended, because he was handsome and energetic and, by comparison, she felt plain. How could he…people must be thinking. I'm amazed that they…Compared to him, she isn't nearly as…

Only once had Hazel and Al mentioned their differences. She had been baking Christmas stretzel, sifting and stirring until lost in a bonnet of flour, and Al had come up behind her, wrapped his arms around her waist, and kissed her neck. For a brief moment, she had wanted to pull away and concentrate on her baking, but just as quickly she lifted her shoulder to pin his face there, and she dipped one floured cheek to squeeze him. After that, Al had stayed nearby while she cooked.

"So who are we giving these delights to? All the neighbors?"

Hazel had shaken her head. "Only Mrs. Palmer. And Phillip's teacher."

"Why only them? Your stretzel is delicious. Bestow it upon the entire city!"

"We'll just keep the rest for ourselves," Hazel had said firmly.

Sitting at the kitchen table, Al had begun to pick candied green cherries out of a bowl.

"We ought to give it away," he insisted. "To the Strouds and the Bestors and the postman and the paper boy. And to that nice lady who does your hair. Well," he interrupted himself, smiling at her dusted form, "back in the days when your hair was brown."

Hazel had looked sternly over her shoulder.

"That's the difference between us, Al. You're generous, open-handed. I want people to deserve gifts but not expect them."

"People have to deserve your stretzel?"

"Yes, they do. And people should work hard, be moral and upstanding. I believe that."

"So do I, my puritan lady, but when that's done, play! And meanwhile, be generous."

"Well," Hazel had said, suddenly filled with envy and shame, "that's you, then."

Al had moved close to her, this time careful not to spot her apron with his green fingertips. "Yes, that's me, a man who needs you just as you are." He had kissed her neck again, and she had wished that she wasn't covered with flour.

Over the years they had melted together, she felt, become more like one another and less like who they had been when they married. Al had become a little less handsome, his ears sticking out more now that he had less hair. After retirement he hadn't insisted on buying a mobile home, and had never, thank God, liked square dancing. He had always been a hard worker, so now he weeded the gravel more carefully than anyone else on the street, and he volunteered to collect signatures for petitions she cared about, or respected the time she spent on some cause.

And she? When she let herself stare into the mirror, Hazel discovered that she had become almost striking, even though her eyes were smaller than she wanted. She was amazed to hear herself chuckle during conversations at a dinner table she herself had set with tall candles and silver and linen napkins. She was amazed to spend money framing one of her own numbered paintings, Al helping her to select the color, encouraging her to spend a bit more than she'd planned. Life with him had been—*fun*, more fun than her parents would have wanted, certainly, but exactly what she'd longed for.

Her mother hadn't come to the wedding; she'd been that mad. Father had, but he'd been so far gone, senile perhaps, that it almost didn't count. He'd blubbered something about Mother really wanting the best for her, but Hazel had ignored him. How could Mother know about the best? A woman who had once been so angry that she had grabbed her child and, red-faced and crazed, sunk her teeth into Hazel's ear lobe and yanked it off. It was a small piece, but enough that Hazel's lobe never looked quite right after that. A mother who could bite her own daughter's ear and let her run screaming and bloody from the house now knew what was best for her? Ha!

Hazel had been right: life with Al had been exactly what she'd needed. Money to take vacations, buy a house just far enough away that she could get to her father's funeral without being expected to bring food everyday for her mother, send their son to college and give him practice in selling and keeping the accounts before they retired to the warmth of Arizona. (She had quietly preferred fog and rain, but to still have Al was good enough.)

And there had been love. More embarrassed by such admissions than he, Hazel had found their 40th anniversary party painful because of the frequent toasts and his pecks on her cheek and the long dance alone out on the floor. But afterward, standing in the hallway outside their bedrooms, she had hugged him tightly and whispered, "I love you, Albert, and I always will." He had squeezed her back. "You'd better, or life'll get awful lonely for me."

Outsiders might not see it, but she was happier than she could have ever imagined when she was a child, fingering the bandage on her ear.

"I thought Phillip was staying!" Hazel cried, looking up from the letter in her hand. She dropped her glasses on their cord and stared at Al across the table. "Why didn't he tell us sooner? What if we didn't want to take care of Mara for a week by ourselves?"

Al shook the paper, then set it down by his cereal bowl. His skin was damp, and he wiped newspaper ink off his fingers onto a paper napkin.

"I was thinking about Phillip while I was showering. This dropping off his daughter so he can take a little trip is typical of him, you know. We shouldn't be surprised. He's always done pretty much what he wanted, him and Loreen. The question is," Al said, dropping the napkin and leaning back in his chair, "what's our granddaughter like now? We haven't seen her since she was a baby."

"That's what I'm saying!" Hazel began clearing away the breakfast dishes, filling each bowl with water before reaching for dish soap. "What if we don't get along? And why Phillip's rush to Sedona? You'd think the place was going to float away." Of course, Hazel thought, that's something Sedona might just do.

Laughing, Al picked up the paper again, turning pages quietly.

"Says here that the school bond is ahead in the polls."

Hazel grabbed a towel and, turning toward Al, began to dry the short stack of dishes.

"Good! Probably had to lean real close to the folks they were polling, tell them to turn up their hearing aids to maximum before they answered the question. Now, if we could just guide their voting hand…"

"Hazel, Hazel," Al said, shaking his head, "don't have such a negative opinion of us older folks."

"Older than who?" Hazel demanded, slamming the cupboard door and folding the towel on the counter. "I don't like this being older, Al. Never have! Inside, I'm just Hazel, with all the interests I had at thirty, but the body won't keep up and I don't like it."

Phillip's letter has made me crabby, she thought, but so be it.

Al reached over to squeeze her hand.

"It's reality, dear. We can't change our age. We just have to keep going the best we can for as long as God gives us. Actually, having Mara visit will probably help us feel younger."

"Or put us in an early grave," Hazel snorted.

She's a pretty little thing, Hazel thought, watching Mara poke through the backyard, stooping over flowers and the dog dish. Long auburn hair and a tiny frame, like her mother, and her father's huge brown eyes and long lashes. She has the small Severn nose. A button, some doctor had called Phillip's, but to Hazel, the worried young mother, it had seemed like her child's body had kept growing long after his nose had stopped, and that's how Mara's looked to her now. But her skin color was healthy, and she ate with proper manners. That's important, Hazel thought, especially for a girl.

The first morning had been difficult, because the child had no preference for the color of her cereal bowl, after Hazel had spent time selecting a good variety. Hazel couldn't believe that it didn't matter, so finally, Mara had blurted out "red!" and Hazel had resolved that that's the color she'd get from now on. No point in going through *this* every day, she thought.

But after that, their time went smoothly. The three of them drove to the brown foothills and hiked along a trail, Hazel naming the shrubs and trees, Mara staring wide-eyed. Another day, Al led them to the shiny City Library, where he eagerly recited the footage, glass and volume figures he'd been told. They packed a picnic to the park, spreading the new red and white plaid cloth over a table before carefully unscrewing jars of pickles, olives, sauce, and then carefully unwrapping a plate of fried chicken. Nervous, Hazel watched Mara's face, but the child seemed willing to eat everything.

"Want Grandpa to push you on the swing?" Al asked, and Mara nodded, her bangs bouncing. Al double-tied her tennis shoes; then they walked to the swings.

Hazel stood nearby, enjoying their laughter, the arc of the swing, the flutter of Mara's skirt each time the swing came down, until she couldn't resist and sat down on the other one.

"I bet I can go higher than you!" Hazel cried and began pumping her thin legs.

"Harder, Grandpa!" Mara squealed, and he pushed more vigorously, turning his head toward the occupant of the other swing. But as she swung higher off the ground, farther from her grandfather's hands, Mara began to whimper, and Al's light taps let her slow down gradually.

"You win, Grandma!" Al laughed. "Come down here. The race is over."

Hazel looked back at them, so far below her, it seemed. Mara stared up, mouth open, fists clutching the chains of her swing, and Hazel extended her legs once again, suddenly enraptured by the height and the power and the ease of it all.

"I should do this more often," she told herself. "It's wonderful! 'How I love to go up in a swing,/ Up in the air so blue!'" she recited.

"Hazel!" Al cried, more sternly this time. As if something could happen, she thought. As if I could be in any danger up here, so close to Heaven. But she began to slow down, to return to her granddaughter, her husband, earth.

The next day the three of them knelt on thin carpet at the Children's Museum and stacked blocks into towers so high that they finally toppled under their own weight. Each time the blocks fell, the three of them laughed. Hazel thought, there's something about all this effort, knowing ahead of time it's for nothing, that's funny. Useless effort strikes us all funny. They wandered around the museum, hardly larger than a store, but they kept returning to the blocks, laughing more loudly each time.

Every evening Hazel gave Mara her bath, Al read bedtime stories, and they both leaned over to kiss her goodnight. Mara grabbed at their necks, murmuring "Night night," and they left her door ajar, tiptoeing downstairs to the living room. Until nearly midnight, they sat, saying little, but more contented in their together-space than they had felt for years.

Al walked into the kitchen, gently closing the door. Mara must be napping, Hazel thought.

"I'll miss her," Al whispered as they sat at the table. "She's been fun to have around."

Hazel nodded.

"It's been nice finding out I can still do things," she said.

"What things?"

"Playing 'Old Maid' or hiking."

Al nodded and stared down at his coffee, his face turned slightly to avoid the steam.

"You know," he said suddenly, "I bet Phillip and Loreen would send her every summer for a couple of weeks. That way they could take vacation trips and she could visit us. What do you think?"

Hazel reached for the earlobe which almost wasn't there, a familiar gesture when she was thinking carefully, and Al waited. Their coffee mugs steamed, the fat clock in the hall ticked loudly, and he waited. Finally, she looked up and pulled on her glasses.

"What's a 13 letter word for 'to put off'?"

For a moment, Al thought, his lips moving in silent counting. Then he answered, "Procrastinate."

Hazel nodded.

"Correct," she said. "So don't deserve the word. Get on that phone and call Sedona."

"You don't think—"

"Listen. You hoped she might make us younger; I was afraid she might be the death of us. We were both wrong. We do better for the time together, that's all."

Hazel watched Al sip his coffee.

"So do it," she urged again.

Al stood abruptly and walked toward the telephone. Hazel watched him, and she thought, so many years, so much kindness. Then, suddenly afraid, she looked down at the newspaper and the crossword puzzle.

Scrapbook, page 2

This page includes two pictures and two pieces of writing.

One picture is of a small house with two lemon trees, heavy with fruit; the other is of a girl sitting on a step, clutching a small dog.

A faded pink thank-you note—"Rough Draft," written in adult hand on the top—is taped next to the pictures.

Dear Grandma and Grandpa, [Mara begins]

> *Thank you for the nise visit. I had a good time. The food was good. We did lot of fun things. I lov you. Mara"*

Centered on the bottom is a school composition, written on lined notebook paper in the script of an older Mara.

I stayed with my grandparents for a week, [Mara writes] *and we really did fill the time. Near the end they gave me a doll with a china face and glass eyes. I could tell I was supposed to really love her and appreciate how old she was. Probably I was supposed to allow her to get even older.*

But she was too stiff, and her clothes were too fragile. On the ride home, I accidentally pushed in her eyes, first one, then, when I desperately went searching for it, the other. Mother saw the doll lying on the back seat and she told Dad. I cried, but they promised not to tell on me. When we got home, we paid to have the doll's eyes repaired, but she's stayed on the shelf ever since.

Did Mara's grandparents pass on something else which could not break? They must have, or the visit would not have been remembered so fondly—by the two older people in the corner of that photo of the house, by the puppy gasping for breath in the girl's hug, by Mara, whenever she pulled blankets up to her chin and, in their absence, told herself a goodnight story.

Chapter 3

"Your grandmother's a real terror at Association meetings, Mara."

Mara looked up from dessert in her grandparents' dining room, evening shadows making the three of them dim gray forms.

"Really?" she asked. "How so?"

Hazel said nothing, carefully sliding her spoon around the bowl's edge.

"She speaks up," Al said, "and the Board isn't used to that. She must have practiced that last speech 10 times before we went to the meeting."

"I did no such thing! Only once!" Hazel exploded. "I have strong feelings on the matter. Who needs to practice strong feelings?"

Al smiled at Mara, who grinned back.

"What was *this* issue, Grandma?"

Hazel looked at her empty bowl and shoved it away so that she could rest her elbows on the cloth, age spots freckling the thin arms cupped below her chin. Truth be told, she admitted, this whole battle with the Association officers was invigorating and she liked talking about it, especially with someone who was eager for details.

"Well, years ago your grandfather and I helped raise money for that nice pool we have at the clubhouse. Olympic size, heated. It's been a real addition to life around here. We have exercise classes and lessons on certain strokes. Even diving practice! Free swimming, of course, which is always popular, especially because of the heat."

Mara nodded, her long hair falling to one side. Hazel thought, what a good listener she is, always has been. Brows pulled together over her nose, eyes holding steady on

Hazel, nodding, asking questions. A nice girl. Good companion for seniors, Hazel thought, and flinched.

"So the Association has a problem with the pool?" Mara asked.

"They have the nerve," Hazel answered, "those men, to tell me that I can't run for an office! And you know why I'm not fit?"

"Why?"

Hazel raised her chin. "Because I'm a *fe*male!"

"What?" Mara cried, and Al chuckled at the two of them.

"Original bylaws," he explained. "Outdated."

"But still active!" Hazel said. "And I won't stand for it! I'm not a feminist, Mara, but this makes me mad. Here I wrote letters, made phone calls, appealed to rich people in country clubs, did everything I could think of because the pool was the right thing, and they don't think I belong on their Board! Where were *they* when the building needed painting? Where were *they* when a lifeguard had to be hired?"

Hazel was angry now, and Al reached out to rub her shoulder, making soothing sounds. Gradually, the flush on Hazel's cheeks faded, and she looked up again, first at Al, then at Mara.

"It's simply a moral question. I'm going to make them see what's right."

Al began stacking their plates.

"The president hates to see your grandmother walk into a Board meeting, Mara," he laughed. "He about has a fit."

Mara stood to help him.

"That fit is guilt. He knows he's wrong."

Hazel remained seated, watching the two of them carry the dishes.

"You're right!" she cried. "Herb Klinger feels guilty. So does that strapping son of his."

"And they ought to, Grandma," Mara said, turning toward the kitchen. "Make them revise those bylaws."

She sounds like me, Hazel thought. I wonder if that's okay?

"So your Government teacher believes in involvement, huh?" Hazel asked as she and Mara folded laundry. The basement was poorly lit but cool as they worked over a long shelf near the old washer and dryer. "I've always wondered why there are more liberal activists—I got that word from Rose—than conservative ones. I'm assuming that anyone who gives extra-credit toward your grade for getting involved in politics must be a liberal."

"Definitely," Mara said, shaking out one of Hazel's wrap-around skirts. "He has a Kennedy bumper sticker."

"Are you going to do it? Work at the campaign headquarters?"

"I was thinking of it. The thing is, I'll need a ride, and Mom and Dad—well, they're Republicans, you know."

Mara hung one of Grandpa's shirts over the edge of the shelf, beginning to carefully button the front and straightening the cuffs.

"They wouldn't give you a ride just because of that? I can't believe it! Your grandfather and I are lifelong Republicans ourselves—"

"I know."

"—but we'd give you a lift to the enemy if you were sure about it. Anyway, I can't stand tricky Dick, so we'll vote Democrat this year." She squinted into the darkness. "Won't we, Al?"

Mara spun around, and Al jerked to a stop at the bottom of the basement stairs, leaning forward into the dim light.

"I just wanted to tell you that I'm going over to the Association office," he called out, ignoring the question. "I'll be back for dinner."

"Who are you voting for, dear?" Hazel asked again.

Al gave a mock salute and turned toward the stairs.

"Don't want to keep you!" he called with a chuckle and disappeared.

"Hard as I try," Hazel said, shaking her head, "I can't guarantee what that man'll do."

Mara stopped folding.

"In a way, Grandpa's going into the enemy camp, isn't he?" she asked.

Hazel shrugged, tossing sock balls into the plastic hamper.

"It bothers me that he still does odd jobs around the Association building, but after all these years, I just have to trust that he'd defend me, even when I'm not around." Eager to deflect the attention, Hazel added, "Does your mother influence your dad?"

"You've never liked Mother, have you?"

Hazel was surprised at the abrupt question, and she looked down at the socks, sorry that the conversation had veered this way.

"It's okay, Grandma. I understand."

"What do you understand?"

"How different you are."

Hazel looked up.

"You're direct and honest," Mara continued, "while Mother says what she thinks will please."

"Well, now."

"And yet, you and Grandpa *seem* very happy."

Mara buttoned another shirt before continuing.

"Sometimes you must try to please him, don't you? Do something just to make him happy or end an argument, that sort of thing?"

Hazel put a hand on her hair, smoothing the sides. It sounded like an awful idea, but maybe she did just slip into that sort of thing without realizing it.

"Your grandfather tries to please me, too," she said. "Marriage should be even." Hazel hadn't known she thought that, but it sounded right, and she repeated it. "Even."

"Oh," Mara said, to Hazel's ears not convinced.

The two women continued folding, the young one working briskly, the older woman more slowly, treating each garment gently, as if it held some story. When the hamper was full and the hangers sorted into a neat row, Mara pulled everything toward her, leaving Hazel with nothing to carry up the stairs.

Really, Hazel thought as she climbed, Mara's too young to know anything about marriage or love. She may be seventeen, but she hasn't lived yet, and those parents of hers—well, even if Phillip *is* my son, I don't understand him. You try so hard and then one day, there your child sits across the table saying awful things, and you think, did I do that? Or he marries some silly ninny and you think, is that my fault? What did I do to make him fall for a girl like that?

By the time Hazel reached Al's bedroom, Mara had already hung up his shirts, so Hazel began to put away the folded clothes, knowing the regular places, while Mara watched from the edge of the bed.

"How did you know Grandpa was the one?" she asked suddenly. "I mean, how could you tell what life would be like with him?"

Hazel thought she looked awfully young, hands twisted between her knees that way.

"You just know that sort of thing, is all," she mumbled.

"But really," Mara persisted, "you could have been wrong. He may not have been anything like you thought, or he may have liked you for all the wrong reasons."

Hazel closed a drawer on the socks.

"Marriage is a gamble."

"I thought you said it's balanced. Even, you called it."

"That's after awhile when you reach a balance. At first it's a gamble, but you're pretty sure it will work out." Hazel didn't like this talk—it was too personal for her—but still, the girl seemed to have questions and shouldn't all questions have answers? "What does your mother tell you?"

Mara looked down at her hands. "We don't talk about much."

I might have known, Hazel thought.

"Look, it will all work out for you. You're a pretty girl, and bright, and someday, you'll just know." Not very convincing. "And he'll know. And there you'll be." Oh, dear.

"How do you stay that way?" Mara asked, her eyes wide.

Hazel picked up a framed photograph, sitting on Al's dresser. It was a picture of Al and Mara at the park, when Mara was only a little thing. Perched on the edge of the sandbox, watching his granddaughter play, Al looked so happy. He held out one hand, pointing toward the camera, encouraging Mara to look and including the person behind the camera as part of his group.

"Marriage isn't death, Mara."

Mara looked surprised, and Hazel sat down abruptly, shocked at her own words.

"I mean, Al liked something about me and I liked something about him, so you basically stay that way. Otherwise, you kill the reason the other person married in the first place."

"But how do you know what that something is?"

What did the girl need? Hazel looked at Mara's wide eyes and tight fingers.

"Well, now," she said, stalling for time, hoping to think of something bright. Suddenly, she stood.

"Why don't you and I drive over to the Kennedy headquarters?"

"Now?"

Hazel smoothed her skirt.

"I'd like to look in there. 'Course, what would they want with some old lady?" She reached out for Mara's arm but then pulled back, shyly. "I'll just have to make them see my value," she said.

Mara smiled. "You've always been good at that, Grandma."

"I gather it wasn't too exciting." Al shook open the paper. Mara already asleep, he and Hazel were sitting in their places near the small fireplace, she working a crossword puzzle with the magazine folded on her lap, he reading the paper, stocking feet stretched out on the ottoman. They leaned toward the light and toward each other.

"It was all right," Hazel mumbled.

"Are you going back? It would seem strange, you not working an election."

Hazel looked up and let her glasses drop on their chain.

"Want to join me?"

"Work for Kennedy? Oh, I don't know. That would seem odd, don't you think? Two old Republicans?"

"I'd like her to see you do it, Al."

"What do you mean?"

"I'd like Mara to see us working together. No," she corrected herself, "I'd like her to hear us discuss it. Talking, coming to a decision. She hasn't seen that work."

"How could that be? She's got parents, and certainly Phillip has opinions."

Hazel frowned, struggling to understand her hunch.

"Maybe Loreen doesn't, or else she hides them. I don't get the idea that they talk much in front of her. And you know what else? I don't think they make her feel very good about herself. They should tell her how pretty she is and smart. Reassure her."

Al looked down at his paper and smiled, wiggling his toes.

"Maybe at her age she wouldn't believe it from them," he said.

"Well, then," Hazel announced, "it's up to us. We'll have to make a more conscious effort at it, Al."

"Tell her nice things?"

Hazel nodded and refolded her magazine.

"Puff her up," she said.

"Easy enough," he murmured.

The two of them, still leaning toward the light, resumed their separate tasks.

Scrapbook, page 3

The photograph, which is large and in color, occupies the entire page. It is of a couple, a man and a much younger woman, the two of them standing outside a small building with "ETERNAL L VE WEDDING CHAPEL" painted in large script above the double door. The chapel is a dirty white, dead vines drooping near a bench which partly obscures a small cross pounded into the ground. The concrete pathway is cracked and uneven, a dry weed growing up through one hole.

Mara is on the left. Hardly smiling, she looks lonely and frightened, as though she had never intended to be here, wearing a lacy peasant dress and a daisy chain atop her long, straight hair. The dress is off-white—is that significant?—and even though she is wearing sandals, the shine of stockings is obvious. Is *that* significant? Instead of a bouquet, she has a wrist corsage, thin and droopy like the vine, and her ring is a narrow gold band, no diamonds, no glitter.

Her bridegroom is grinning broadly, his hand high on her side, the fingers curving beneath her breast. He has deep wrinkles around his mouth and eyes, and his hair is wavy, thick and dark, like a movie star's. Perhaps she fell for the hair, for the control and maturity.

If she does not want to be at this chapel, would she rather be at a church somewhere else? Would she rather be wearing a more formal gown, her family posing around her? Her father, mother, wishing her well, waving goodbye? A minister giving his blessing? Would the marriage work out better with a change of place for the ceremony, a greater expenditure of effort?

Or perhaps the ceremony should never have occurred anywhere, at any cost. Perhaps Mara should be posing without the corsage in front of Bridal Veil Falls in Yosemite, a simple tourist traveling with friends. Perhaps what this picture really shows, if one bends close to the faces, especially the eyes, is that these two were not made for each other, that the young woman is trying too hard and the man accepts that as his due, that their lives will never find an even balance.

If this is so, then the photograph is not a memento of a celebration; instead, it captures a tragedy. One wants scissors or a thick pen to damage the faces or to at least add a ring to the groom's finger. "ETERNAL L VE WEDDING CHAPEL" becomes more than ironic; it becomes Truth.

Scrapbook, page 4

This page is missing some items, yellowed tape left flapping, and the holes through which a gold rope twines are torn, letting the page hang at an angle. But two items do remain:

In the bottom left corner is a photograph of a grinning Mara, stretched out in a hammock. One knee is raised and an arm bends over her head. Her fingers wear no rings. She is wearing white shorts and a white blouse, knotted above her waist, and she is tanned a rich brown. Behind the hammock is a palm tree, a small piece of ocean and fluffy clouds in a blue sky. If the person stretched out in the foreground were not recognizable, the photo could be an ad for some retreat, some far-away island paradise. Perhaps it is.

The setting and the grin revealing her dimples make her a very different woman than in the previous picture, the wedding pose. Here she looks confident, even a little sexy. She looks comfortable. She is not frightened by the camera or by the person holding it. She likes herself.

So then it did turn out all right? Was that face on the page before just youthful shyness, normal apprehension for a new bride? No. Consider the only other item on this page.

It is a letter, in tidy, dense handwriting on faintly lined stationery.

"Dear Mara, [Al writes]

"Your grandmother and I are both terribly sorry that the marriage didn't last. It had seemed a bit fast, but then, we're out of touch and thought

perhaps long courtships are old-fashioned these days. Certainly, not everyone starts out smooth-sailing, but it sounds like you had more than your share of problems. No woman should have to tolerate what you did, and we don't blame you for taking action.

"When you get back, please visit. It's been too long since we've had a good talk by the fire, you helping Grandma with her crossword puzzles. Speaking of who, she wants to add a note—

"Darling, [Hazel writes, in remarkably similar script, just a little larger]

"Grandpa is right, no blame here. Tell your parents phooey from me. You did the best you could and now you've learned about yourself and you won't make that mistake again. Isn't that pretty good, not making the same mistake twice? This world needs more people like that.

"By the way, city incorporation passed. I don't know if Al voted for it, but I think he did.

"Rose sends her love. She doesn't know the whole story, but I'm sure she'd send her love anyhow. Let's hope you're not pregnant.

"Love,
"Grandpa and Grandma"

Perhaps the love in that letter is why Mara is smiling in the photo. Perhaps she has just received it, torn it open quickly, and begun to feel more warmth than from the sun. In the gentle breeze moving the palm fronds, she throws back one arm and swings the hammock, contented that she has, at least, one home.

Chapter 4

"Why go back to school, Mara?" Hazel asked, cutting her pork chop with effort. "Criminey," she mumbled, "my arthritis must be bad tonight."

"It's not you," Mara assured her. "My knives are dull."

There was silence for a moment as they ate. Both sat with their chairs close to the table, knees almost touching under the drape of a linen cloth. They were actually eating in Mara's living room—the apartment was small. But the large windows which looked through a patio and garden filled with bougainvillea out to a range of purplish-gray mountains, that view plus the thick walls, Mara had told her grandparents, were enough to endear the place to her.

"Anyway," Hazel finally said, "do you need more training to keep your job?" She'd never understood this training business, having been employed by her husband in their own store, but she'd heard that employees had to upgrade their skills or risk losing their jobs. Would someone consider firing her Mara?

"I could stay a paralegal forever, Grandma, but that's the point—I don't want to. Teaching is for me. I just know it."

"So you need what degree?"

"A Masters for now. Eventually, maybe a doctorate."

Hazel nodded and chewed, then raised her head abruptly. Behind the glasses, her eyes were wide with alarm.

"You're staying around here, aren't you? You don't have to go somewhere else to get these degrees?"

Mara smiled as she stood to refill the basket of rolls.

"Don't worry. The University has all I need."

"Good. I admit we'd be sad if you had to move." Sad is hardly the word, Hazel thought.

"You're both important, you know," Mara said quietly.

Hazel looked away.

"Oh, not important. We're just—"

"No, I mean important to me."

Hazel flushed and began sliding items on the table, trying to distract herself as well as Mara.

"Well, now…" she muttered.

Mara threw back her head, laughing as she sat down with the basket.

"Grandpa's right! You always say 'well, now' when you're in a corner!"

Hazel pursed her lips, then smiled. "Your grandfather talks too much. By the way, how's that Richard fellow? We enjoyed his recital. We don't listen to classical type music very often, but he seemed good. The audience liked him."

"He got a good review in the local paper. See it?"

Hazel shook her head.

"But good local reviews don't make a big career," Mara continued. "What he needs is something from New York, Los Angeles, some big metropolitan center."

"And meanwhile?"

Mara stared at her plate, brows drawn together.

"Meanwhile, he teaches."

"That's a comedown? I thought you were looking forward to the job."

"That is because," Mara said, enunciating carefully, "I cannot play an instrument. If I could, then I'd rather perform than teach others how to. I'd rather be famous myself than help others be famous."

"Is that how Richard feels?"

Mara shrugged. "I'm not sure, but I think so, if it didn't sound so horrible to admit it."

Hazel pushed back her plate. "Not horrible."

"Ambitious then. Selfish. Something like that."

A moment passed before Mara spoke.

"Richard tries to be a good person. Unlike someone I was once married to."

Hazel was startled. She had never liked Dom, but this business of having discarded mates…Better not to refer to it.

Mara changed the subject. "So what are you up to these days?"

Relieved, Hazel answered with energy.

"Well, I don't know if you've seen any lately, but comic books have gotten out of line. Way too violent. They certainly shouldn't be sold to children. So Rosie and I started sort of a lobbying group. There are about eight, ten women, old friends mostly, and they meet in my house, write letters, call store managers. That's what I'll be doing tomorrow."

"Have you had any luck?" Mara asked.

"Some. One manager agreed not to buy any comics next month."

"Grandpa said Reverend Bolt mentioned you in his sermon last week. He said people shook your hand as you left the church."

Hazel bit her lip. Al was forever building her up.

"Embarrassing, that's what it was."

"But well-deserved."

Mara set coffee in front of her and poured in cream.

"Your such a dynamo, Grandma. I really admire that. All that involvement keeps you young, don't you think? I mean, look at both of you. Aware, concerned. That must help avoid all sorts of problems."

Hazel chuckled.

"Al says mostly he naps. He says it's something he does better than golf, bowling, almost anything. Some people just have a natural talent for napping, he says, and he's one."

"Of course, he'll never be praised from the pulpit," Mara laughed. "Quiet talents like napping just don't attract the attention that telephone campaigns do."

"He says his skin will stay lovelier—it's true! He said that!"

"Well, after all, Grandma, what matters more: a child's clean mind or a man's smooth skin?"

As they laughed together, Hazel was surprised at the sound of her own voice. I guess with Al I'm mostly quiet because we know each other so well by now, and with others I'm serious because projects have to get done. Only with Mara do I laugh. Amazing.

The party *is* a hit, Hazel thought, just as Rose had said. She'd drifted by like some pink chiffon cloud on no other than Dade Williams' arm, and I suddenly felt frumpy. Rose always has that effect on me. From where I sit, hidden by leafy ferns and bougainvillea, I can watch them dance. Look at them tighten their arms around each other as though they, not Mara and Richard, had just promised to love and honor each other, as though all these people had come to smile at them, as though anyone here even cares who they are!

Thinking of that, Hazel looked back toward the apartment and watched her granddaughter shake hands, hug laughing friends, even loosen Richard's tie. He wasn't possessive about her, Hazel thought approvingly. They're close but easy and I like that.

But I want to leave, she thought. I'm happy for Mara, and happy that they'll live nearby as they go to graduate school, teach, however they plan to spend their days. I like Richard. I trust this one. It will last. Poor as church mice, maybe, but it will last.

No, she thought, I want to leave because the bursitis in my shoulder aches, and because I don't drink, and because the food's too salty. Mostly because I've never liked parties. Laughter and music and good times make me feel nervous, as though I don't deserve to have fun. Keeping a serious face helps avoid being cursed by the Fates. I've always been that way.

"Want to dance, my lady?" Al's voice whispered. He gestured toward the patch of lawn where Rose and Dade were no longer the only couple. "I can't say that they're playing our song. Come to think of it, do we even have a song?"

Hazel shook her head and fingered the jade bracelet on her wrist.

"You know I can't dance, Albert, so why do you ask?"

"Because," he said, bowing low, "I want the challenge of persuading you. Dance with me, Hazel. Please."

When she began to finger what was left of her earlobe, obviously considering the request, he repeated, "Dance with me. Give Mara that pleasure."

"Well, now," she muttered, and he lifted her elbow and led her to the lawn, where they moved together awkwardly, unaccustomed to the position.

"I'm glad you joined us!" Dade's voice boomed out. Hazel saw couples begin to dance where they were standing, near tables or potted plants. Everyone could take only tiny steps before dancing into some object, so her own halting movements with Al bothered her less. When the music stopped, she looked at Rose, who was staring into Dade's face, and she felt annoyed.

"Are you happy?" Al asked, leaning close. "Because I am."

Hazel looked away from Rose and said gruffly, "That's because you've had too much champagne."

"I haven't had any," he answered, beginning the next dance by tightening his right hand against Hazel's back. "Mara's happy. She's married a nice boy. Rose is happy. She thinks Dade loves her, and he may think so, too. And

I'm dancing with the only woman here who doesn't look silly."

Hazel felt peculiar, as she always did when Al referred to her as a woman, and she unconsciously lowered her forehead against his shoulder. He backed her away from Rose and murmured, "Perhaps the only real woman period."

Looking up, flushed and feeling very peculiar now, Hazel frowned over Al's shoulder.

"Oh," she said, "this old striped thing."

"You look like you're having a good time," Richard said to Hazel. They were standing together in the small kitchen, Richard wrestling with champagne bottles and Hazel arranging crackers on a platter of cheese.

"I am," she said, ignoring her bursitis. "It's a nice party and you had a lovely ceremony."

Richard grinned proudly, and Hazel thought again what a nice man he is, even if his hair *is* awfully long.

"When you two were standing up there, I realized how you have the same color hair, just the same. And I was struck by how much taller you are—at least four inches! Why haven't I noticed that before?"

"Because," Richard said with such a straight face that Hazel simply stared at him, "most days I don't wear such high heels."

Hazel quickly looked down at his feet, but he put his arm around her, laughing.

"What's so funny?" Mara asked, appearing in the kitchen doorway.

"Nothing," Richard said, kissing Hazel quickly on the cheek, "just noticing things. Like your parents, for example—" and he turned toward where Phillip and Loreen sat. "Why does he keep looking at his watch? Could he possibly want to leave?"

"Don't worry about it. They're just jealous." Mara kissed him, only his cheek but firmly, leaving him with a pink smudge. "Don't you agree, Grandma?"

Before she could answer, Richard asked, "Why would they be jealous?"

"Because I'm happily married and they're not. It's hard for parents to see their offspring being wiser than they are."

Mara looked at her parents, sitting silently. Her father turned to Loreen and said something lost in the music.

She may be right, Hazel thought. I wouldn't know. We never feared our son was making better decisions than we had, although certainly he's made more money, if that means much.

"Wiser, unh?" Richard smiled over his champagne glass as he took some cheese off the platter Hazel was working on. "Does that mean you've decided?"

Mara didn't answer.

"I notice the woman who would be your dean is here. That's a good sign."

Shaking her head, Mara said, "She's just on vacation."

"Still, they must want you. And I'm game for the move. I know a few people in L.A."

Mara looked through the glass doors toward the dancers, her eyes following the couples as they moved in such a cramped space.

"Really," Richard persisted. "They're smart to want you."

Mara shrugged.

"Well, now," she said, and Richard threw back his head in laughter.

"What's so funny?" Hazel asked, turning from the counter. She'd been trying not to eavesdrop, trying not to panic at the thought of Mara moving.

"She sounds just like her grandma!"

"So soon?" Hazel's lips quivered as she risked what she considered an off-color joke. "You've only been married a few hours!"

Looking between her husband and her grandmother, Mara raised her champagne glass.

"Well, now!" she toasted.

Suddenly, Al was at Mara's elbow.

"May I have the honor?" he asked. "Hazel has warmed me up, so I'm in good shape."

As Mara began dancing with her grandfather, Hazel watched.

Dancing's not so bad, she decided. Maybe we should take lessons. When Richard cut in, Al smoothly turned to embrace Hazel, and she gripped his shoulder more tightly.

Scrapbook, page 5

On this page are a diploma, a letter, and a tiny envelope. The diploma is from the University of Southern California, and it includes a gold seal holding down an inch of shiny red ribbon. Mara's name, centered on the paper, is written in graceful calligraphy. Made on ivory-colored linen parchment, the diploma deserves to be framed, but instead it is mounted here with small, black picture corners, a sign that it is not important, rarely needed.

Overlapping one side is taped a letter from Hazel.

Dear Mara, [Hazel writes]

Your grandfather and I are as fine as could be expected, given how ancient we're getting. Al complains about his arthritis more, and bills from the drugstore are higher than we can afford, but I won't kick him out just yet. Especially since my bursitis is acting up so bad that I may have to buy a sauna or go in for regular massages, which aren't cheap. Why does this aging business have to cost so darn much? There's a lot to be said for just drifting away on an iceberg.

Glad you found a house and you like grad school. In that order. Where you spend most of your time is more important than classrooms. Now that you've graduated, will that school hire you? I mean, can you just stay on and switch from student to teacher? That would seem reasonable, since they know you.

You say that Richard is doing some playing for studios. You mean Hollywood? Should we be looking for his name at the end of movies? Not that Al and I go out much, but it would be nice to see a familiar name. Tell us if you're going to be on the Oscars. I'll call all my friends, even ones in the grave. Might give them a lift.

We miss you, but you know that.

Love,
Grandma

P.S. Grandpa sends his love, but you know that, too.

The small, tan envelope has typed on the front MARA LEEDS—KEY—HOWARD 200. It is missing the key, which is in use or returned or lost. The faint drawing on the envelope is the USC seal, so Mara must have obtained a job at her alma mater. She must have begun to teach, to discover the joy of shaping a presentation, the frustration of facing a class which does not value her knowledge as much as she does. Since she saved the envelope, this job must have been significant, if sometimes disappointing. Like the symptoms of aging, she might have realized—unavoidable.

Chapter 5

"You know what I just may do?" Hazel asked, looking up from her breakfast. Her hair was completely silver, still drawn back into a tight bun, and her reading glasses hung on the same chain. "I think I may try my hand at some stretzel again."

Al didn't look up right away, which bothered her. He'd been drifting off like this for several weeks now, with a far-away gloom on his face, and barely eating a thing. When he napped, he closed all the curtains and slept for hours. This wasn't her Al.

"I could send some to Mara for their first holidays in their new place, and to Phillip—that was something I cooked which he actually liked, if I remember right. What do you think?"

Al blinked at Hazel, then looked back at his oatmeal.

"Oh. I don't know. Seems like a lot of work."

Hazel leaned over her own empty bowl.

"What's the matter, Al? You don't seem yourself lately."

Al shook his head.

"I'm all right."

"You aren't." Hazel insisted. "Let's go see the doctor."

Al stared at her.

"You make it sound like a field trip," he said.

Hazel smiled to hide her fear.

"Think of it that way. A red popsicle if you're good. I'll call."

She started to rise.

"Sit down, Hazel. There's no point in wasting the money."

"It's not a waste!"

"It is. Whatever I've got, I don't want to mess with it."

Hazel grabbed his hand.

"What do you mean, whatever you've got? Tell me what's wrong!"

Al shook his head and stared down at his oatmeal, a drying mound in a puddle of milk.

"Nothing needs fixing, Hazel."

To Hazel, his voice sounded like the oatmeal, bland and cold and lacking any vitality, any life. Abruptly, she rose to her feet.

"I'm calling the doctor."

"No—" Al protested, but she had already begun to dial.

What happened next she could never remember with any clarity, and that bothered her, because she fancied herself an intelligent person, aware, verbal enough to make herself understood. But after the doctor's visit, Al was swept away from her, and she could never get enough answers. "We're running tests," they said first, and then, "Waiting for the results," or, "More tests." She spent days, it seemed, waiting in rooms with uncomfortable chairs, filled with families who didn't care about understanding, or in hallways without chairs, in the way of employees.

She almost dreaded visiting Al's room, because he was often groggy and when he wasn't, he expected explanations, which she couldn't give. It was a horrible feeling, to have gone against his wishes, delivered him up to some monster system, and then failed to protect him, failed to justify what she had insisted upon doing. She felt confused, and she didn't like it.

Going home was almost worse. Every light bulb chose this moment to burn out; faucets which had never leaked dripped water now; weeds sprouted tall in the front gravel. Their low-maintenance, retirement home was suddenly making demands, and that was exasperating.

"You know I can't do anything about you!" she yelled at the furnace, fat and quiet, no pilot light flickering in its grayness. "Well, I'm going to go lie down, and you'd better fix yourself before I get back," and she slowly climbed the basement stairs, aware that she was being illogical but unable to stop herself.

Rose took charge, sending Dade over to repair, to water, to fill up the gas tank so Hazel could drive between an empty house and the crowded hospital. After a week, Rose went with her and tried to intercede.

"It's hospital policy to talk only with family," the nurse told her.

"But I'm as close to family as anyone in this town!" Rose cried. "His poor wife isn't clear about what's happening, and I thought—"

"Excuse me," the nurse said, pulling the folder from underneath Rose's arm. "If you'll have a seat, I'll call the doctor."

Rose took a deep breath.

"Dr. Allen to Waiting Room 4. I'll just stand here until you broadcast that."

The nurse frowned at Rose, a small mole almost disappearing in the crease near her mouth as she pursed her lips.

"That won't be necessary."

"Nevertheless," Rose said, "I'll wait."

The nurse leaned over, pulled down a switch and clearly enunciated the call. Then she looked up at Rose.

"No need to look so proud," Rose said, turning toward the chair where Hazel waited, watching her. "After all, you're just doing your job."

When Dr. Allen appeared in the doorway, Rose jostled Hazel into standing and walked with her.

"My friend needs some answers," Rose prompted, poking Hazel's back.

But Hazel twisted away from Rose's fingers, and Dr. Allen took a step sideways with her. Hazel noticed his white hair above the starched uniform and pale tie. Well, she thought, at least the doctor's experienced. I don't want anyone practicing on my Al.

"You're Mrs. Severn. I'm Dr. Allen," he said, tipping his head slightly. "Wouldn't you like to sit?"

"Actually, I'm tired of sitting," Hazel said. "Have all the tests come back yet? Do you know for sure what he's got?"

"We think so. He has cancer, Mrs. Severn." And he pronounced a part of the body which Hazel knew nothing about, had barely heard of.

Groping behind her for the wall, she found instead Rose's arm. In a moment, sitting down and staring at the floor tile, she felt steadier.

"What can you do about it?" she asked.

Dr. Allen told her what they were trying, the names of medications, and how long Al would be on each one. He even explained about the tube they had put in his arm, what it had in it, why it was helpful. He talked for quite awhile, but she was basically not listening, waiting only for him to pause.

"All I want to know is, will he get better?"

For a moment Dr. Allen was silent. Their two faces looked at each other: eyes darted across the opposing face, searching and assessing.

"I can never say. Patients always surprise me."

If she had wanted an answer, Hazel had lost.

"But there's—there's no guarantee?" she asked.

Dr. Allen shrugged and patted her hand.

"I simply can never say. Let's just take good care of him, all right?" and he stood.

Waving aside Rose's arm, Hazel walked to Room 17 alone. She wanted to stare hard and see for herself. See what? she wondered, pushing open the door. See determination? Strength? Some hint of the vital man she had always lived with?

But what Hazel saw was sickness. There he lay, pale and shrunken. One thin arm, lying on top of the sheet, was connected to a tube, and strange machines stood nearby, not yet needed, she thought, but waiting. Hazel sat heavily in the only chair and reached out for his hand, covering it with her own and lowering her head. He didn't waken, and she stayed, bowed against their hands, until a nurse came in to turn on the light for evening.

At first Hazel sat by Al's bed each day, but a nurse took her aside and said that some patients, especially men, prefer privacy.

"They're used to being strong for the family," the nurse said, "and they just can't be sick. I'm not sure we do them any favors by staying close."

She made sense, and after that, Hazel didn't go back to the hospital as often. If Al had spoken, or if she'd been asked to do something, then she would have felt necessary, but she couldn't sit by a lifeless *thing*.

"That's all he is," she said to Rose. They were organizing bills at her kitchen table, being old, Hazel called it. "I don't think he recognizes me anymore. Yesterday I signed some papers against forced feeding, special equipment, things like that."

Rose looked alarmed.

"You don't want them to try everything? I would!"

Hazel smiled faintly.

"I'll remember that, Rose."

"Have you called Phillip? Or Mara?"

"I talked to Loreen last night. Phillip's in Japan somewhere, but she'll tell him as soon as he calls."

"And Mara?"

I feel guilty about this, Hazel thought, because it's not the right thing to do. I know it's not.

"You've called Mara?" Rose persisted.

"I haven't told her," Hazel answered softly.

"Why not?" Rose cried. "She'd want to know."

Why not, Hazel demanded of herself, but she couldn't picture Mara without seeing Al, seeing all three of them together, and she couldn't stand it, being only two, not yet. It was easier, somehow, having Rose around, less painful.

"I couldn't handle it if Mara wanted to be here," she said finally.

"But she wouldn't have to stay *here*, if you don't want her to! I'd take her. I have plenty of room."

"Somehow…I don't know." Hazel spoke so softly that Rose had to lean forward. "I just can't tell her. I don't want to hear myself say the words."

"His illness would seem too definite?"

"His death. There. I said it." Hazel dropped her head onto her hands but didn't cry. Rose wiped her own cheeks with a flowered handkerchief.

"You've had so many years together," she said, dabbing the last damp place on her cheek. "Someone wrote in to Abby and said that divorce is a better way to end it, so instead of being sad, you're just mad…Wouldn't that be easier?"

Hazel looked at Rose and thought, how stupid. She may be my friend, but she's dumb.

"I feel both, Rose, sadness and anger. Right now, mostly anger."

"But why would you be mad at Al? Or you mean the hospital?"

"Him. He's leaving me."

"But you still have a son." When Hazel waved one hand, Rose said, "All right, then, you have your granddaughter."

Hazel twisted her coffee cup.

"She has her own life now."

"Well," Rose cried cheerfully, "then you have me!"

Hazel stared at her, circles darkening the skin under her eyes and silver hair coming loose from the bun. You're it? she thought. After 80-odd years, you're the best I can do?

That had been the wonderful thing about Al: he'd made her feel like a better person.

"Thank you, Rose," she said firmly, "but I'll manage," and she lifted her chin to the ceiling, eyes closed.

"I'm glad you were there, Mara."

Mara sat in Al's wingchair, staring at her hands, saying nothing, so Hazel took her time arranging the afghan over her knees. Perhaps I can ease us past these moments by making a few harmless motions, she thought.

"Do you remember that park?" she asked. "They've built a nice little Memory Garden, haven't they? Grandpa would like being there."

Nothing. Could she be mad at me? Was I that wrong not to tell her?

For a moment Hazel watched the log burn, and she felt slowly better. All the chores surrounding a fire—carrying in a few logs, arranging the kindling and paper, sweeping the hearth and setting the screen just right—I shared those chores for so many years with a thorough and patient teacher, the best. And now here I sit, bringing that warmth into my home for the first time in months. Normality. Routine.

"I wish I could have said goodbye."

Hazel turned quickly, but Mara remained staring at her hands, and Hazel wondered if she had dreamed the remark.

"Squeezed his hand," Mara said and looked up.

"I'm sorry," Hazel murmured. "Maybe it was selfish of me."

"Were you with him?"

Hazel nodded.

"And it was peaceful?"

Hazel nodded again, then took a deep breath. I haven't said this to anyone, she thought.

"I saw his soul float away. Float up from his body and evaporate through the window. Do you believe that could happen?"

Mara looked toward the fire.

"It's been a comfort, remembering that," Hazel continued. "Somehow he feels closer. I could even let Rose clean out his bedroom, pack up his stuff for the Goodwill because he isn't there anymore. Does that make sense?"

Mara still quiet, Hazel carefully folded her glasses on the end of their chain and allowed her mind to wander. I can still see Rose, she thought, shaking out Al's fancy business suits, dumping drawers onto the bed, leaning out the window to yell at Dade to hurry with the extra boxes. Even after Al's room was empty, it didn't hurt to stand in the doorway because I could feel his soul in the air above me, and I just knew that he was too special to be held down by clothes. Except the lamb's wool coat. I did save that, at least for now.

Clearing her throat, Mara said, "This is going to be a shock for Dad."

Hazel sighed.

"No one thought he'd be so hard to reach."

"And Mother's sick."

Death is never convenient, Hazel thought. It doesn't check to see if you're ready, doesn't make sure the timing's all right.

"Are you going to be okay, Grandma?" Mara asked.

"Oh, I'll be all right. I was thinking I might move to the Bay Area. We lived there once, a long time ago. I liked it." Hazel laughed softly. "Your grandfather didn't much care for the fog. He liked heat, sunshine."

"Do you have friends up there?"

Hazel shook her head, then reached up to touch what was left of her ear.

"I'll manage," Hazel said, picturing herself walking along a damp hill, wearing Al's coat.

Mara leaned forward.

"What did you say?" she asked.

But the lump in Hazel's throat made it difficult to speak.

Scrapbook, page 6

A page is completely blank, clean. Nothing has ever been pasted on that page—no remains of tape or torn photos. No dried streaks of glue. Nothing, as though skipped deliberately, left as an offering, a memorial, a blank tribute.

Scrapbook, page 7

But this page is a sudden riot of color. In one corner is an orange airplane ticket, showing that Mara Leeds flew a three day round trip to San Francisco just before Christmas. Next to that is the royal blue stub of a car rental receipt, so that Mara can move from the airport to perhaps the snapshot of a green apartment building: The Gables, reads the chunky letters across the front of the building. From the metal supporting the canopy at the front door hang large pots dripping with fuchsias in reds and pinks. An enormous velvety fern almost blocks the door handle, and along the path are pansies growing in a tumble of color. The top right window is open and a form is barely visible there, waving a slender arm toward the camera.

The photo below shows Hazel with glasses hanging from a chain and silver hair drawn back from her thin face. Her hands are clasped awkwardly in front of her skirt, and she is wearing a black sweater, too thick for the flimsy fabric below. Unsmiling, she looks preoccupied with something off to her right, as though impatient with the photographer for bothering.

Also on this page is a small greeting card, the cover a painting in browns and beiges of the Madonna holding a happy, chubby baby. Inside Hazel has written,

Mara—

When the fog really settles in, I feel cradled like this infant. This place suits me just fine. Glad you like your new classes and Richard's doing well. Facing my first holiday without Al, but so be it.

Much love,
Grandma

The last item on this page, in the middle on the left, is a gift tag, the small square type with a tiny hole punched through the corner so that a thin piece of red thread can poke through and tie onto the package's ribbon. Hazel's handwriting, although always tidy, is very cramped, and she can barely squeeze in her message:

Gpa. would be happy if R. got use out of this coat. Love, G.

Carol Huebner

II

Gertrude Dunzler

Chapter 6

"Hurry in!" Gertrude Dunzler called to Mara, cheerfully waving her down the slippery rock steps to the arched front door. "Come in out of the rain!"

Mara jumped across a puddle in the moss and almost sprinted through the open door, which made Gertrude laugh as she hung Mara's raincoat on an antique rack. Her wispy silver hair flew in untamed curls around small brown eyes and a long, slender nose, and her cheeks flushed with pleasure at welcoming a guest.

"Oh, I do admire the litheness of youth!" she chuckled. "Litheness. Is that even a word?" But she didn't wait for an answer. "Here, you rest while I gather the tea things."

Mara half rose from the small chair with its ornate wooden back, her hair damp above her sweatshirt.

"May I help?" she asked.

Gertrude waved her aside.

"On some later visit, but today you are grand company! Honored guest! Guests remain in my parlor, waiting to be served. They do *not* discover the mess in my kitchen! That is for old friends, which you shall become soon enough."

They both laughed, and Gertrude hurried into the kitchen, arranging on a silver tray the items she had readied earlier: two floral cups and saucers, sugar cubes in a silver bowl with tiny prongs, a tea pot with steam drifting from the snout, and a small platter piled with Christmas cookies and slices of pound cake. She placed the tray on a table next to Mara and sat in the opposite chair.

"How beautiful!" Mara exclaimed.

Gertrude smiled proudly as she poured the tea and offered sugar.

"Life needs these small graces, don't you think? So much tribulation that the spirit is replenished by even brief moments of civility."

"I hadn't thought about tea quite that way," Mara said, "but you're right."

Gertrude lifted a cloth napkin to touch the corner of her mouth.

"People assume that elderly ladies living alone have no interests and certainly little beauty in their lives. Bah! That only proves how dangerous it is to base conclusions on superficial evidence. As my Fritz always used to say, 'Build on sand, beware of water.' Or something like that."

He used that expression a lot, Gertrude thought, especially about our neighbors. I wonder why it's a bit of a muddle in my head.

Mara smiled and gestured toward the platter.

"You have lovely things," she said.

Gertrude nodded.

"Silver is terribly time-consuming to keep clean, but it's worth it. I must say that I have trained my girl well. She calls herself a cleaning lady—can you imagine? Lady! Her husband Clyde picks her up here in an old Cadillac. We didn't even own a Cadillac when my Fritz was alive, and we certainly would have suited it better than she does. But coloreds like big cars. Fancy motors to make them feel important, don't you think?"

Mara carefully set down her cup but said nothing. Gertrude extended the platter.

"Would you care for some pound cake? It's Van de Kamp's. That's the only decent brand and nice cake does add so much to a tea. I always tell Lucy to buy it, but I can tell when she skimps. The texture is different."

"Delicious," Mara said.

"Lucy isn't even much good at cleaning," Gertrude continued, carefully breaking the thin slice of cake in half, "but she's been with me for years, and there is such a thing as loyalty, wouldn't you agree?"

Gertrude waited and Mara asked, "How long has she worked for you?"

"Long enough," Gertrude answered. "In the beginning, she tried to call me Trudy, but I put a stop to that. I may be elderly, but I will not be patronized! We compromised on Mrs. D. You may call me that also." I'm glad to have names out of the way, Mrs. D. thought. If it's done early, it lays the proper groundwork. "And your husband is Richard?"

"Yes."

"No children?"

"No."

"Not *yet*," Mrs. D. corrected. Bearing children is the main reason women exist, she thought, and I cannot imagine what else any young woman does with her time.

"Perhaps not ever," Mara smiled. She has pretty eyes, Mrs. D. thought, and such lovely auburn hair. Her husband has the same color. Their children will be beautiful.

Mara gently lifted a cookie. I wish I could have baked my own, Mrs. D. thought, instead of serving Lucy's. They could be store-bought and here I am, offering them on a lovely plate, for all the world as if they're elegant. Well, I won't mention it, and perhaps Mara will never notice.

"Tell me about your work. I only know that you teach."

Mara sat back on her chair.

"I teach American Literature plus I help with the newspaper."

"I just love literature," Mrs. D. said, dropping one sugar cube into her cup, "and I do believe in being well read. My son Nelson is an editor. Did I tell you?"

"Of a newspaper back East."

"The Philadelphia Globe," Mrs. D. nodded. "Such a fine writer, and knowledgeable about everything. I always enjoy reading his editorials. His wife clips them and sends me a bundle every month. Where are you teaching, dear?"

"At City College."

"My goodness! They teach literature there? That hardly seems to be what those children most need." Like teaching Shakespeare to my Lucy! Mrs. D. thought. What's the point?

"City has a very good English Department," Mara said, "and an excellent newspaper. It ran a series on different celebrations associated with the holiday season which was really well done."

The two women sipped and ate in silence, Mrs. D. not choosing to respond. The comment was, after all, about religion. Along with money and politics, those three topics are better left unmentioned.

"Why did I think you taught at USC?" Mrs. D. asked finally.

"That's what Mrs. Peterson said when she introduced us, but I'd left there when they wanted me to get a doctorate. I really do like where I'm teaching, and I like the campus, the whole environment, actually."

"That's very brave of you," Mrs. D. said.

Mara was silent for a moment.

"Brave?" she asked.

"Working in that area. Someone has to do it, I suppose. And your husband?"

Mara chewed carefully before answering, her eyes slightly squinted and her cheeks flushed.

"I have many bright students, Mrs. D. Some of them are every bit as smart as students at USC, but their families don't have enough money, so they go to City. Its school paper staff turned out more professional journalists last year than the USC Trojan."

Mrs. D. looked away, her eyes drifting around the living room, trying to find a new topic. This neighbor might turn out to be a bit brittle, she thought, avoiding glancing at Mara's chair. I hope she's not like the Petersons. They're raising four unruly children right next door to me, with all the fights and loud music. At least Fritz and I were able to shape our son's temperament. That's an important part of being a parent. Mara's wrong to think she can avoid the responsibility of motherhood. Well, these days maybe she *can*, but she ought *not*.

Suddenly, her eyes lit on a brightly colored card propped against a vase.

"My grandson sent me that Christmas card," she said. "He has real talent, I think."

Mara turned to look and smiled.

"It's darling," she said. "And I didn't say how much I like this room."

Mrs. D. smiled in return, and both women continued commenting on pieces of furniture and decoration, standing to look more closely. When they went upstairs, Mrs. D. held the banister tightly.

"I hardly ever come into the rooms up here," she said, stroking the heavy curtain in a room filled with a sewing machine, ironing board, worktable, scraps of old patterns and folded bolts of cloth. "Since I set up a bedroom on the entry level, I rarely need anything up here, and Lucy dusts only if I remind her. Look in this closet—" here Mrs. D. opened a small door—"at my damask cloths. Aren't they lovely?"

She touched each cloth gently as she spoke.

"This one was always used at Christmas, with one of those lace cloths draped on top. Mother brought out her finest china, and Jeffrey—he was our manservant—arranged fresh holly. After my father lit the tall red candle sticks, my parents stood at either end of the table and we all held hands—I had two brothers and a sister, you know—and we said grace, very soft, very solemn. Oh—" Mrs. D. shook her head quickly— "dining was so elegant at Christmas."

Mara nodded and listened as Mrs. D. described other linens, what tables they fit, when they were used. By the time Mara was pulling on her raincoat, she was holding a small doily, very old, Mrs. D. had told her, and one of a pair made by an elderly aunt.

"You keep that," Mrs. D. said as she patted Mara's shoulder, "and I'll search for the second one. Who knows what I may find in the process?"

Laughing gaily, she waved Mara up the rock steps to the winding street.

As Mrs. D. cooked a simple dinner, most of it from frozen packages, she thought over tea with Mara. The girl is really very nice, she thought, attractive and well-bred, except for a few disturbing attitudes, but then, young people these days have to be forgiven such slips. Generally, she's a good addition to the neighborhood and who can tell? Visiting occasionally, sharing a refined tea and conversation about world events, might help to soften Mara's edges a bit, make her a better wife to that nice-looking young man. What did she say he did for a living? Mrs. D. couldn't remember that they'd discussed it, although she knew she'd asked the question, such information being in the category of vital.

After dinner, Mrs. D. went gingerly up the stairs for a second time that day, clutching the railing with one hand and steadying herself against the wall with the other, determined to find the other doily, even if it meant unfolding, unstacking, rearranging. I'm not comfortable with the idea that Mara might think things are lost in my home. Like my son or his wife writing that I should move into a retirement home because the house is probably getting beyond me. Nonsense. Nothing of the sort.

As she opened the linen closet, she suddenly thought that Mara might find associating with an older and wiser lady, someone of taste and culture, someone well-read and well-informed, she might find such an acquaintanceship—no, better yet, a friendship—appealing.

She definitely might.

Scrapbook, page 8

Winter things on this page:

A card shows Mara and Richard, arm in arm, grinning happily in front of their home, the eucalyptus trees shading where they stand on the front porch. Next to the photograph is a printed Christmas message, wishing friends well from their new address.

Below the card is taped a yellowed, crocheted doily. Amazing, incongruous to see such a thing mounted in a scrapbook! Fluted edges extend from the tight circles at the center perhaps three inches, making the doily a possible cushion for a delicate vase, a picture of one's spouse in a silver frame, an open bowl of licorice buttons for little fingers. Any of these items would hide the small glob of red nail polish, which mars the weave. Overlapping one corner is a piece of ivory-colored stationery with "Gertrude K. Dunzler" lettered in brown across the top.

Dear Mara, [Mrs. D. writes]

Good news! I found the mate of the precious doily I so grandly presented to you after our pleasant little tea. Please forgive my hasty wrapping in an obviously once-used box—my regard for you is not nearly so worn, I assure you!

We must share tea again soon. Since the climb up the hill is difficult for me, I trust that you can once again visit my humble home. Until I call to make the arrangements, please think of me fondly as—

Mrs. D.

And overlapping the other corner is a small, white index card with an explanation typed by Mara:

Since I have two [Mara writes]—*and really don't need either—I'm putting one in here. To have a large collection of such things, to have used them regularly, and to feel so obviously proud—how different life once was. Spending time with Mrs. D. is an adventure into another era and another lifestyle.*

Finally, in the top left corner is a faded newspaper clipping. Rare snow in parts of the Los Angeles basin, the article says, caused accidents, frantic emergency calls, power outages and at least one grand snowball fight, atop Griffith Park in a parking lot near the Observatory. The picture is of a crowd of children and adults dressed in warm clothes, throwing hastily packed snowballs at one another or sliding on frozen puddles or cupping mittens around their mouths to yell at someone outside the photograph, hidden behind a car or a tree trunk. The snow could not last long, and there is a desperate look in their faces, a hasty eagerness even in the eyes of Mara and Richard, the couple in the foreground who are having splendid fun for a short time.

Chapter 7

"You have to live more frugally, Mother," the woman said, carefully closing a cupboard. "Your Social Security increase was minuscule and still you live high."

"High?" Mrs. D. cried. "You call frozen meals and half a package of cereal for breakfast *high*?" The idea! Mrs. D. thought. As though after visiting once a year Louise knows how I live! She is only, after all, a daughter-in-law, not even my own flesh. How dare she give advice!

"I'm not referring to your eating habits," Louise said. "But, for one thing, you use too much gas and electricity."

Mrs. D. made an exaggerated shrug.

"I don't see a single light on."

Louise remained standing at the cupboard.

"You heat your kitchen with your oven, Mother, and as soon as it starts to get even a little dark, you turn on all the lamps, even the outdoor lights!"

This is outrageous, Mrs. D. thought. Outrageous and rude.

"Look at my hands," Mrs. D. said, holding them toward Louise. "Do you see those blue veins? I'm always chilled, because at my age, my flesh is thin. So I do the best I can not to freeze to death. As for the lights, do you begrudge a woman making her home a bit welcoming?"

"Welcoming?" Louise repeated in disbelief. "Welcoming to whom?"

Mrs. D. smiled.

"One never knows," she said and looked at her lap.

Shaking her head, Louise walked to the sink, where she had to push two sleek, black cats off the counter before she could make room for her dish.

"Your animals are another thing!" she grumbled. "How many of those creatures do you own?"

Mrs. D. wondered at Louise's annoyance.

"One never quite owns a cat, you know," she said and thought, animals soften a place. They make a home, the way children's laughter does.

"But how many are yours, Mother?" Louise asked.

"Oh, three, perhaps four if you count Colonel, but he's rarely around."

"Were they strays?"

"Every one abandoned," Mrs. D. announced.

"Are they all neutered?"

"Such a question!" answered Mrs. D., flushing. "Of course, they are! I would always do the responsible thing for animals."

"How?"

"Excuse me?"

"How have you gotten them to a vet to have them neutered?"

"A neighbor."

"This Mara person?"

"Usually."

"That's very nice of her. And the expense? You've had to pay for those operations, I assume."

Mrs. D. straightened in her chair.

"I have a very kind vet who doesn't charge me the full amount. He knows how hard I try to be *frugal*."

There!

Louise turned back toward the sink, suds bubbling over her wrists, and worked quietly. Watching her, Mrs. D. thought, I don't like the gray—it doesn't suit her skin and besides, it makes *me* feel old, seeing my son's wife gray. And that style—short and straight—is really no style at all. I must remember to discuss hairstyles with Mara. That would be a fun topic.

Louise dried her hands and pulled a chair out from the kitchen table.

"I'm sorry," she said and leaned forward earnestly. "I don't mean to be critical," she said. "Nelson and I are glad you have company, but we worry about you, living here alone, lighting the oven for heat, catching assistance where you can."

"I pay Lucy, and Mara helps out of kindness."

"Of course," Louise said and hesitated. "Mother, we've always been honest with one another, so let tell you frankly what worries us."

Here it comes, Mrs. D. thought. The Penultimate.

"We worry about your expenses. Since Nelson handles your checking account and pays the bills, he can see that you're using up an awful lot of your savings. One day, your savings will be gone, and frankly, we can't handle our bills plus yours, too. If you want to live in your own home, you'll just have to…"

Mrs. D. sat quietly, looking at her lap and not quite listening. My diamond is so pretty, sparkling against my dress, she thought. But it's small, and that makes me feel sorry for Louise, for Nelson, for the whole family. I'm even a little cross with Fritz. He should have left us better fixed. I would have made a fine wealthy dowager. I have all the right tastes in music and art and certain ecological causes, and I would have been beneficent with my money, funded endowments, read my name in bronze letters on the lobby wall of a hospital or theater. As it is, here I sit defending the expense of neutering cats.

"Let's end this discussion, Louise," Mrs. D. interrupted quietly. "I know what you're saying, and I'll try to stay within my budget."

As Mrs. D. rose, Louise extended a hand.

"I'm sorry," she said. "I didn't intend to sound so—so—unchristian."

Mrs. D. smiled faintly.

"Just don't let the cats hear you," she said, and they both walked into the living room with their teacups.

Intending to send some pages back with Louise, Mrs. D. sat down to continue her memoirs for her grandchildren. For some months she had been painstakingly composing with a fountain pen on white bond paper. Nelson had suggested that she tell about her life so that her grandchildren would become better informed about an earlier era. Every few months she mailed several more pages filled with her flowing script, each paragraph beginning with a large swirl and the margins occasionally decorated with tiny drawings. Each month she hoped for a thank-you, but after the first note, the children didn't write again. Mrs. D. kept composing, enjoying the memories about her childhood, her marriage, her life in Hollywood.

She could still remember the day they had bought this house. Another reporter had told Fritz that the place was perfect and it was—its slightly Victorian look, two large fireplaces, black and white tile counters and bathrooms, and leafy views—all perfectly charming. The only problem was buying it for a price they could afford, and when it seemed that the owners were stubborn, they offered more than they'd planned: fourteen thousand dollars! What an unthinkable sum! But the owners offered to leave their houseplants, and Fritz' job seemed permanent, and it was beginning to look like they'd have only the one child, so they did it. How exciting it had seemed, and how reassuring when Fritz' judgment turned out to be, once again, quite right.

Fritz was five years older than Gertrude and such a brilliant man, such a fine writer. She remembered lengthy dinner table lectures about current events, especially FDR, and gradually, as Nelson grew old enough to follow the news, the two men began to converse. They were both Republicans with a conscience, she liked to think, cautious about finance, but liberal in advocating social justice, particularly if it meant a better prospect for business. As she spoke less, she found herself actually forming fewer opinions, until, finally, Fritz had two votes in every election, marking her sample ballot before they drove to the polling place. Never three votes, though: Nelson took after his father in holding strong views.

After Fritz had a serious heart attack, he came home from the hospital to recuperate in their bedroom. Every morning she'd bring in the paper, fix his breakfast tray, and, while he ate in bed, sit on the trunk at the foot of his bed, reading aloud the articles he wanted to hear. Gradually, she began to care about current events again, and by the time Johnson became President, she had formed her own views on conservation and the space program. Fearing that her opinions might create a disturbance, she said nothing to Fritz.

One day she climbed out of her bed, glancing quickly at his form while she pulled on her robe and went down to fix his breakfast. It was a cold morning, so she made oatmeal, trying to stir so that the spoon didn't clang against the side of the saucepan. On sudden impulse, she opened the back door and cut a leafy fern growing near the step and stuck it into a small vase. Newspaper neatly folded on the tray's edge, she returned upstairs to their room and set the tray on the trunk.

"Breakfast time!" she cried gaily and touched his shoulder. "It's so foggy outside, the paper's a bit damp, but we can still read it."

Fritz didn't move. She touched him again, then pulled the sheet away from his face.

"Wake, up, sleepy head!"

Then she saw that his mouth was hanging open, and a tiny line of saliva was dangling from the corner. But it was his eyes—his eyes! They were looking straight at her, but not seeing. Impossible, she thought, sinking back onto her own bed and clutching her robe. He's dead! My God, he's dead!

She reached for the sheet and pulled it up again. As long as he was staring at her, she couldn't think, and she must think, she must be clear about this. During the night he had…his heart had…perhaps if she'd stayed awake, she would have heard something, might have called an ambulance, the paramedics. But she had slept. How could she do that? After so many years, wouldn't she feel something was wrong, sense a faint message, know that he was signaling for help? How could she sleep while her husband died in the next bed?

Turning away, she doubled over and twisted her hands tightly while her lips moved in prayer, but she did not cry. Even later, as she searched through her closet and her drawers, looking for somber colors to match her mood, her face was wooden. How could she tell their son? And what would she do alone?

After she'd dressed, she sat stiffly in their bedroom for a long time, waiting to accept that Fritz was not going to prop himself up against the pillows, unfold the paper, and ask why she'd picked the fern.

Lucy had packed Fritz' things for the Goodwill. While Mrs. D. had sat in the sewing room, calling out advice, Lucy folded and sealed, gradually emptying his half of the closet, the shaving things from the medicine cabinet, his four drawers in their chest. Suddenly, she marched out of the bedroom, holding up a long strand of pearls. Hanging at the bottom was a heart-shaped emerald surrounded by diamonds.

"What—" Mrs. D. gasped. "What is that?"

"You can see what it is, Mrs. D. I found it in a drawer. Could he have been fixin' to give you a present?"

Mrs. D. felt her heart beat faster.

"In a drawer?"

"All laid out in a velvet box shoved way back behind his shorts. Isn't it beautiful?" She moved her arm up and down so that the emerald swung in the light.

"You shouldn't be playing with it, Lucy!" Mrs. D. yelled, grabbing the necklace from Lucy's fingers. "You still have a lot to do!"

Lucy frowned and reached one hand to her throat.

"I was just showin' you what I found."

Mrs. D. looked at the necklace in her hands.

"Well, I have it now, so you can get back to work," and Lucy walked off.

He knew I don't care for the green of emeralds, Mrs. D. had thought. And this necklace is so…flashy. I could never have worn such a necklace, never have had the clothes or the occasion, let alone the desire. Mrs. D. tried to remember any time when she may have admired an advertisement or a jeweler's window, but there was no such memory.

Fingering the pearls like a rosary, she suddenly knew that the necklace had not been meant for her.

Quickly, her mind was filled with overlapping images of the corpse on the bed in their room, the paramedics and ambulance, the minister and the service and the graveside. In those hectic days, when she hadn't been her most observant, was there a grieving shadow of a woman, hiding behind a black veil? Perhaps a bouquet from someone unknown, some woman he'd met while researching a story? Someone who might suit these?

After Lucy had gone for the day, her husband honking the old Cadillac as they rounded each corner on the narrow road, Mrs. D. climbed the stairs to her bedroom. She dropped the necklace on Fritz' bed and sat on the trunk for a long while, not so much thinking as editing mental pictures: posing for their Christmas card with a baby, smiling in a Venetian gondola, toasting an editor, eating alone when Fritz was out of town. The necklace changed everything somehow, made her feel stupid, then angry. While I waited for him…Was it because I couldn't…? How often had they…?

Just before she switched off the light, she grabbed the necklace and dropped it into one of his empty drawers. Later, she must decide what to do with it, how to get rid of it in an acceptable way. Not at a pawn shop, not that sort of place, but sell it or give it to someone.

Or perhaps, she thought, pulling the bedspread up to her chin, I should simply pretend I never saw it.

Mrs. D. felt proud as she folded yet another few pages for Louise to carry to her children. Here I am, widowed for five years, and managing just fine. Nelson and Louise had thought I'd have to move into an apartment or some retirement home, but they didn't appreciate what strong stock I come from and how resourceful I can be. It was simply a matter of paying Lucy to come every day—she likes having the work and at least I can do some small thing to help the coloreds. Here in my own home I have opportunities—to save cats, to form opinions on neighborhood activities, to be a gracious hostess—and what is the point of life if not to make the most of opportunities?

Mrs. D. caught sight of herself in the small mirror next to the front door and touched the waves at her temples. She admired her hair, so perfectly colored and shaped at the salon. I look like someone who has had advantages, she thought with some pleasure, and perhaps should have had more—wealth is so often wasted on those who can't use it well.

I hope my grandchildren and some dear friends, like Mara, feel I've added to their lives. Goodness knows, within my limitations, I've tried.

Scrapbook, page 9

Something has spilled on this page, something once a bright yellow but now rubbed dull. As though to emphasize just how dull, a bright orange telephone message is taped next to the smear. The printed heading says CITY COLLEGE and the message is printed neatly.

Mara, [the message reads]
Tuesday, 3 p.m.

A 'Mrs. D.' called. Apologized profusely for using your work number. Isn't well. Wonders if you'd stop by on your way home. Please please. Sorry to bother. Sorry sorry.—J.

To have been saved, this message must indicate something. Was it Mrs. D.'s last telephone call, her final words mocked by some unknowing clerk? (Typical, Mrs. D. would say. What can one expect? Still, we must try.) But no, there is another message in the same handwriting.

M—
Mrs. D. again. (It's been awhile! We had a nice chat— weather, illiteracy, grim job market.) Hates to bother you, but Lucy left her w/o milk. Could you pick up some? Many many thanks from her as well as the cats.—J.

And then a newspaper article about—perhaps this is not so amazing, considering that Mara assembled this scrapbook—an article about cats and the benefit of giving them water, not milk. The writer is identified as a veterinarian, and the picture accompanying the article is of a fluffy Persian-type cat, very pretty and contented-looking, dipping over a bowl of milk, its tiny tongue curled back to make a spoon. The caption says that an old wife's tale has been proven wrong, but next to that is Mrs. D.'s flowery script:

No matter what the experts say, cats will always love milk!! How could what we love be bad for us??
Next to her response is a small square of yellow paper bearing Mara's handwriting:
Chocolate,
Daily champagne,
Fascination w/ Kennedy assassination...
To name only a few fond things which could be very bad.

This is a lively page. It could have a title: CATS! or MESSAGES! Mara was careful to save these scraps from her daily life, to assemble them so that they could reveal the natural flow, the small truths. Perhaps such things were not visible to her until, putting aside the glue and pens, she suddenly saw the page come together, saw the simple patterns of life. Then she might take a moment to smile and to be glad for what she had seen.

Scrapbook, page 10

In comparison to the previous page, which had a theme, this page appears boring. It contains an airline ticket and two postcards.

One is of downtown Los Angeles with five skyscrapers and puffy white clouds against a blue sky. The card is taped only along the top, so that if you fold the card back and turn the book around, you can read the other side. It is addressed to Mara at some hotel in Denver, Colorado, and the message reads:

How long did they have to wait to get such a clear photo? Just to remind you of home—
Love,
Richard

Below it is an extra large postcard of the Rocky Mountains, addressed to Richard in Hollywood, and on the back, Mara's message, neat in black ink:

Dear Richard—[it reads]

My speech was a success! And the conference is excellent. I'm really learning a lot about working with "disadvantaged youth' and feeling affirmed in my direction. The mountains are a beautiful daily backdrop, but I'd take you and good ole' LA any day. Much as I'm enjoying this, I can't wait until Saturday.

Love,
Mara

Glued to this page *could* be an article on romance, or perhaps what it takes to create a long and loving marriage, or a wise exchange between Abby and a reader. *Could* be but is not. Richard and Mara have not been married long enough to be self-conscious about their love. Nor are they old enough to be grateful. They simply enjoy each other's company, and they would rather be together than anywhere else, no matter how much attention that "anywhere" might offer. They have other passions, but they care most of all for one another, and perhaps that will always be, perhaps not. Who can predict about anyone's life?

Chapter 8

"So tell me about the conference."

Mrs. D. and Mara sat at Mrs. D.'s small kitchen table, the sun hot on the table's vinyl surface. Mrs. D. wore a housecoat and slippers, and her hair was straight and drab— she hadn't felt up to the salon lately. It's best, she'd decided, rather than pushing myself to dress for the salon, just not to look in the mirror.

"Years ago I went along with Fritz to a few journalism conventions and they were really grand events, especially for the wives. Tours and informative talks. I imagine Denver was lovely."

Mara nodded.

"Beautiful. Someone had a car and on our last day we drove into the Rockies for a picnic at the Great Divide. The view was spectacular." Mara leaned close, with a conspiratorial grin. "We wasted a bunch of wine, testing which side of the Divide it would run down."

"I hope the wine was inexpensive."

"Screw-top bottle," Mara assured her, and they both laughed. "But the conference speakers were all excellent, some really big names in education."

"How stimulating," Mrs. D. smiled, taking a small bite out of a cookie on a plate between them. "I love Denver. We went through there on a train trip years ago."

"How did you end up living in Los Angeles?"

"Job, I suppose. That's so often the reason, isn't it? An important editor had read Fritz' articles and hired him. Then there was the baby and the house and before we knew it, years had passed! I never intended to stay here."

"You don't like it?"

Mrs. D. shook her head, tapping the napkin to a corner of her mouth.

"This place isn't me, dear. I was born in Massachusetts and raised throughout New England—my father was a popular economist, you know. Radio broadcasts, articles, university positions, that sort of thing. During my youth the West was thought of as heathen territory, populated by Indians and cattle drives, so I thought of visiting it only as a tourist." Mrs. D. looked out the window. "Sixty years later, the tourist remains."

"What about joining your son?"

"I could never live in Philadelphia."

"Why not?"

Mrs. D. poured herself more tea and extended the pot toward Mara, who shook her head.

"Being a parent is not easy, Mara. What's called for is the constant use of discretion, so that you see but do not comment, and at this distance, I see less. It's much easier to be discreet when the parent is separated from the child by three thousand miles. I believe he loves his mother, but he might not if he had to see her often. By the way, you told me some time ago that you hadn't definitely made up your mind about having children. Have you considered it further?"

I won't remind her, Mrs. D. thought as she leaned back against the chair, that some time before *that* she had said absolutely not. Foolish conviction but some progress made.

Mara blushed and fumbled with her cookie.

"Well, actually…"

Mrs. D. clapped her hands.

"You are with child! How splendid! When is the happy day?"

"Mid-July."

"I'm delighted! I can keep my windows open and enjoy baby sounds. Now—" Mrs. D. rose, steadying herself for a moment before walking toward her small bedroom off the kitchen— "I've been saving a few of the books I used as a young mother, just in case."

"Oh, you really don't have to—"

Without turning, Mrs. D. waved aside Mara's words.

"At my age I don't *have* to do anything. That's one of the few benefits. You just stay there while I find the stack." Her voiced fading as she moved further from the kitchen, she called out, "They might be a little dated, but I always say that knowledge never goes out of style."

Re-emerging in the doorway, she stood holding three dusty, brown books.

"My own son rejected that advice when he became a parent, and what does he have to show for his views? Two children who refuse to do chores or homework. So listen to me, my dear: good discipline is based upon knowledge, and knowledge is fundamental to our culture."

Mara smiled but said nothing. I think she agrees, Mrs. D. thought.

"You have an obligation to sustain the culture."

Again there was silence, and Mrs. D. wondered if keeping one's own counsel avoids rudeness or rather creates the suspicion of it.

"I hope these help," Mrs. D. said, putting the books on a small table near the side door. "You'll do a good job, I have no doubt about that. And what a nice change of pace for you, after years of keeping such a frantic schedule. Not that a child doesn't make demands, but a mother at home is up to any challenge."

Mara cleared her throat.

"I'll be going back to work in the fall."

Mrs. D. was startled.

"Which fall?"

"When the baby is two months old."

"But—who will care for your child, if not its mother?"

"Richard will take some time off. He's eager for the— the change of pace."

Mrs. D. stared at her cup and at the plate of cookies. I've heard of this trend, she thought, being a working mother, the father more involved with child care. Somewhere I've read about it, or Louise mentioned it. It's apparently increasingly common, but so different from my years with Nelson!

I fed him with tiny, engraved spoons and bathed him several times a day and kept his linens clean. So much of those first years was involved with keeping everything clean, especially so that Fritz wouldn't see any changes in our lifestyle. When he did, when I was frazzled or breathless or the living room was messy with toys and discarded children's clothes, I saw Fritz frown and I knew that after dinner, or perhaps even before, he would disappear into his den or drive off into the darkness, and I'd be left rocking my son and singing lullabies—alone.

Now here's a young woman saying that her husband *wants* to stay at home. How can that be? And isn't the woman better fit? Isn't she the one a child craves?

But honestly, Mrs. D. admitted, whenever Fritz came into the room, Nelson's little head turned so eagerly, pulling away from my breast or, later, from his truck, or his coloring book, or his desk. When I walked in, he sighed. So perhaps it made no difference that she had always been around when he was an infant.

Suddenly, Mrs. D. felt very tired, and she was glad when Mara stood to leave.

"How are you feeling?" Hazel asked, glad for the sound of Mara's voice.

"I can hardly breathe, Grandma. The other night Richard and I went to one of those restaurants where you sit on cushions and eat with your fingers. After a couple hors-d'oeuvres I was full, and a sip of wine made my heart beat like mad! The doctor says another two or three weeks, but I'm ready now."

"Pregnancy is too long by about a month. The nursery's set?" I'm sure it is, Hazel thought. Just like me: organized, prepared.

"All but the diapers. They arrive next Monday."

"A diaper service, then. I like that. They didn't have such things years ago. I had to scrub Phillip's diapers by hand, and I never could see that it made them any cleaner. Do you want a son or a daughter? And don't give me any of that 'It doesn't matter, so long as it's healthy' stuff! Everyone has a preference."

Mara laughed.

"I admit I'd like a son."

"You do mention your male students more often."

"I do?"

"Probably because they have more interests than girls, stronger personalities."

Hazel wondered where she'd heard that. From Mara? That would be embarrassing, saying it back to her, except that at my age I don't need to be embarrassed about anything.

"I'd raise him to be a good babysitter, though, and he'd learn how to cook and clean," Mara assured her.

"The wifely arts. And his name?"

"We're not sure of the first, but I think we agree on a middle: Albert."

Hazel was silent for a moment, tears coming to her eyes. Al was suddenly back in the present, after she'd been trying so hard not to dwell on him, rarely mentioning things they'd done together and never quoting him. Widows at the church so often began their sentences with, "As my dear husband used to say…" and it bothered her, especially when she knew for a fact that the husband had been buried for fifteen years.

"Albert' is awfully old fashioned, Mara. You don't hear it much these days."

"So much the better. It adds integrity."

Integrity—such a strong word. Well, let Al back, smuggled carefully into a middle name, she thought.

"What about if it's a girl? And don't say 'Hazel'—that's a hideous name, one I'd dearly love to dump."

"Too bad when they marry, women don't drop whichever name they'd like to get rid of."

"That would've been a tough decision: Hazel or Landover. Both awful. So what name will a daughter have to live with the rest of her life?"

"Maybe Katherine."

"Katherine. I like that. I could call her Katie. Would that be okay with you?"

"Of course!"

"My best friend when I was little was named Katie. She had long, red braids, and she always got A's in school without ever studying. I think later she had a crush on Al."

"But you got him."

"She ran off with some fellow who joined the army and was killed in the war. After that, I lost track of her. Anyway, you'll have interesting children," Hazel said.

"Children plural?" Mara laughed. "You sound like Mrs. D. She's already got me being the stay-at-home mother of a whole flock!"

"But I thought you like your job."

"I do. I'm not going to stay home, Grandma. I'd go crazy."

"I felt that way, but it wasn't common then, and people didn't like it when I set up Phillip's playpen at our store. Don't you worry about what anyone thinks, Mara. Don't even read the books. Just trust your instincts. Use your common sense."

"Actually, I *have* done a lot of reading. Mrs. D.'s books are pretty dated, but we've bought some newer ones. I think we'll be fine."

"Mara, listen. Reading doesn't matter on this one. Every time we talk, you tell me about how you've practiced pant-blow or you're going to have dim lights or whatever. But labor is not an intellectual experience! You know what it is? Tell me a seven letter word for 'hang in there."

Mara offered an immediate answer. "Cope isn't long enough. Survive?"

"Survive. That's your goal. That's sort of all you ever hope for with children."

"Their survival or yours?"

"Both!"

Hazel hung up a few moments later, still shaking her head but smiling because, worried or not, she knew Mara and Richard would do okay.

Scrapbook, page 11

In the center of this page is a 5x7 photograph of a baby, bald and vacant, like so many newborns. On the corner of the picture is a tiny blue ribbon, a wordless confirmation that Mara did, indeed, have a boy. He's lying squarely in the center of his crib, tightly wrapped in a pastel receiving blanket patterned with tiny giraffes and butterflies.

Who does he look like? Bald and body hidden, it is impossible to tell. Nothing about his features is yet firm. The baby announcement, the list of gifts, the description from the mother's Journal of his delivery, none is here, all presumably tucked into their proper albums.

The only other thing on this page is a photo, which must have been rejected from a more formal place. It is not flattering: Mara has a weak smile, a double chin and snarled hair, and the high metal sides of the hospital bed look imprisoning. Richard is gripping one bar, staring open-mouthed at the photographer, his eyes baggy above a wrinkled gown splashed by a jagged coffee stain. The new parents, in one of their rare, childless snapshots, look not joyful, not blessed, not overcome by tender emotions, but downright haggard. Especially their eyes show that they have experienced something for which they could never be completely prepared, and that is a humbling experience.

These two pictures—one of the new infant on his fresh sheets, wrapped in a never-before-used blanket, the other of the stunned parents—must capture the reality of parenthood for Mara. Her eyes are different—sadder. Lettered across the bottom of the page are these words: "LABOR IS NOT AN INTELLECTUAL EXPERIENCE."

Chapter 9

Mrs. D. sat awkwardly in one of Mara's teak living room chairs, not comfortable in this environment of Scandinavian furniture. Spartan, she thought, not quite welcoming. But she had prepared for coming up here, making an effort to match her dress and shoes. She hadn't brushed her hair, leaving wispy curls flying at crazy angles.

"Thanks for walking up, Mrs. D. It's hard for me to get away."

Mara sat on the couch, buttoning her shirt after nursing her son whose chin was damp and shiny below heavy eyelids. Lifting the limp bundle onto her shoulder, she began to pat his back lightly. Mrs. D. breathed more easily now that Mara was modest again.

"I admit the climb wasn't easy, but Lucy helped part of the way," Mrs. D. said, "and I did want to see you and the baby. How are you feeling?"

"Tired," Mara admitted with a smile.

Mrs. D. nodded and smoothed her skirt.

"The only way around that is to have help. Your mother couldn't stay?"

"Only the first two weeks, and we didn't wake her at night. Matt has another month of having his own way, and then I'm back to work. I'd love it if he'd sleep through the night by then."

"I'd have to check those books, but don't I remember something about a bottle close to bedtime? Or cereal? When does that start?"

As Mara continued patting, Matt's head hung heavier against her shoulder.

"I'll have to check, but I think it's about then."

"And are you determined to return to that job? I understand that's how it's done these days, but if you could afford—"

"We could afford, but I'd be miserable," Mara said firmly.

"Miserable taking care of your baby?"

"Miserable. I'll be an excellent mom—for about five hours a day."

Mrs. D. didn't join in Mara's laughter. Instead, she picked a piece of lint off her skirt before looking straight at her young hostess.

"Sometimes," she said, "I think that young women these days have too many choices. If you didn't have an easy option of working, then you'd make your peace with mothering. You might be the better for it, and certainly your child would be."

The two women sat silently. Watching Mara's face, Mrs. D. was sure that her young friend felt turmoil inside. She doesn't look quite sure of herself or of this darling little boy she's carrying to bed. Well, that's enough for now. When she comes back, I'll change the subject to more neutral territory.

"When do you think you'll be able to come down? I want to listen to a new tape Nelson sent me."

Mara stretched before turning to Mrs. D.

"Tape of what?"

"A new singer, Placido Domingo. His voice is incomparable, I've been told. Do you know opera well?"

"Not at all. Richard says that's a real flaw in my character."

Mrs. D. chuckled. She always liked what Mara told her of Richard and regretted that she had only limited conversations with him.

"He's right, but tell him that I'll remedy your character."

After checking the baby, they walked carefully down the road, Mara holding Mrs. D.'s elbow and pointing enthusiastically toward wild flowers until, half way back to her house, Mrs. D. waved Mara off her arm and continued alone.

"How lovely to hear from you, dear!" Mrs. D. said into the telephone. "I just read through all the items in a thick envelope from my Nelson and I'd wanted to read you the editorial he wrote on Viet Nam—well, the Domino Theory, actually, and how it may not be true. Will you be down this afternoon?"

Mrs. D. carefully transferred the pile from her lap to the small table near her elbow.

"Actually, no," Mara answered, "that's why I called. I have to get ready to go to Portland tomorrow."

"Portland! Oregon or Maine?"

"Oregon. That's where—"

"I lived for a time in Portland, Maine, you know. Junior high school, I think. I loved Maine. Beautiful countryside, especially in the fall. Oregon I don't know at all. Why are you going?"

"My father died this morning."

Mrs. D. stopped short. She had been talking, gibbering, Fritz used to call it, while this poor girl was bearing grim news.

"Oh, I'm so sorry, my dear. How did it happen?"

"Heart attack as he was getting out of the shower."

She sounds calm, controlled, Mrs. D. thought.

"You've never mentioned your parents, Mara. Were you very close to your father?"

There was silence, then a quiet "Not really. But this is a shock."

"You probably have a great deal of unfinished business with him, and now it's too late."

I read that years ago in "Atlantic Monthly," she thought, and it always seemed so true. Sudden death sets the head spinning, because we expect everyone around us to live forever, to keep doing what they've been doing, so we don't tie up loose ends. We don't think to take a close look at what is.

Suddenly, she saw herself holding a long strand of pearls with an emerald catching the sunlight, and she looked away from the memory toward the reality of a cat jumping onto her kitchen counter.

"When is the service?" she asked.

"Thursday. I'll be flying up with Matt."

"Take care, my dear. My condolences to your mother."

"I'll call when I get back," Mara said, and the conversation ended.

"Well, it was a nice service," Hazel said, setting aside a plate of sliced ham and scalloped potatoes, and looking at her great-grandson in Mara's lap, his tiny hands clasping a bottle but his eyes darting to each figure in the room. "But I'm glad Matt's too young to understand. Just blobs, that's all he knows."

Mara looked down and smiled fondly.

"Blessed innocence."

"It doesn't last long enough," Hazel said firmly. "Too soon we get hurt and then, if we live long enough, we feel loss. I hate it."

"Loss?"

Hazel shook her head until the chain holding her glasses tapped against her cheeks.

"Outliving everyone. It isn't fair, you know. First Al, then Phillip. They've left me and I don't like it one bit." Hazel leaned forward, shaking a finger. "Death is so—so…selfish!"

Mara shook the baby bottle slightly.

"They knew you'd do okay, Grandma. You still have the Sunday School job, don't you?"

Hazel told herself that Mara was preoccupied feeding the baby, which was annoying. One more person thinking only of her own little world.

"Sunday School! Except for me, no one reads to those children, and it's criminal!" she cried. "They have such inquisitive minds, just going to waste! They need stories! They need models! Whatever's going to become of them?"

Hazel knew that she sounded cranky. Maybe that's what living alone does, she thought: you get stubborn, opinionated. There's no one around to challenge you just by the way he brushes his teeth or ties his shoes. Then you get pushed out into some social situation—if a funeral could be called that—and you discover you've become crotchety. Hazel didn't like that, and then she thought, Good Lord, now I'm cross about being cranky!

Looking around the room, she realized that, apart from Mara and Loreen, she didn't know a soul, not one of her son's friends and especially not the business associates. My life is really separate, which is—no, not fine, but just the way it is.

Gently withdrawing the bottle, Mara set it on the table and lifted her sleeping son onto her shoulder.

"One day," she said, "not long after Matt was born, I was rocking him in the living room, and I realized that if someone came bursting in at that moment, some burglar with a gun who said, 'You child or your life!' I'd be willing to die to save him. I mean, even though I love Richard, I'm not sure I'd die for him, but I would for my child. That's the first time I ever felt that way."

Hazel stared at her granddaughter.

"No one ever gave me the chance," Hazel said suddenly. "I would have made the switch. I mean, a parent should never outlive a child. Never! What am I supposed to do now?"

Mara tightened the blanket around her son.

"What you've always done, I guess. Stay involved, stay connected."

"Hmff!" Hazel scoffed. "Easier said than done."

Matt had begun to cry, and Mara stood, saying over her shoulder, "What else is there?"

Seeing her granddaughter tending new life bothered Hazel.

"I don't have much choice, do I?"

She grabbed her plate, spearing the wide slice of ham with her plastic fork and shaking it from side to side. This meat is Al, she thought. It's Phillip. It's everyone who's gone before and left me here, telling stories to kids in a dingy room behind a church. Well, when I go to my Reward, I'll sit on a sofa with Al nearby, and I'll do crossword puzzles for eternity! No one better ask *me* to get up, because I won't do it. I'm just going to sit there with a magically sharpened pencil and fill in all those little squares. Forever.

She watched Mara dangling napkin shreds, trying to entice Matt's tiny hands to reach for something and distract him, but it didn't work. Matt wailed and Hazel smiled. A five-letter word for funeral song, she thought. D-I-R-G-E. Not a pretty sound.

Scrapbook, page 12

In the top center is the second page of a letter to Mara from her mother. Perhaps page one said affectionate things, depressed things, trivia about cleaning or the weather in Portland, but we will never know because Mara chose to tape here only a page marked "2." It is cream-colored, linen-weave, and Loreen's handwriting is narrow and small.

"At any rate [Loreen's page two begins] *half a year is too long: I'll move next month. (I'm sending a picture.) Grandma Hazel might be pleased that I'll be close, although her note refers only to her church, so I'm not sure. It will be nice to live with my sister's family and be able to visit old friends. They'll all take good care of me. Plan to visit. Richard is welcome and, of course, my grandson.*

Love,
Mom

To the right of this page is a photograph of a sprawling white house, landscaped and carefully tended. An arrow is drawn to the far window below the words MY ROOM. No faces appear in this picture, no human life, no colorful plants or drooping vines. It is as though Loreen selected a pristine environment, almost a nunnery.

Below the photograph, apparently not related to it, is glued a telegram from a garbled address of mainly numbers, only one word recognizable: London!

Richard—[the telegram reads]
Hurry! Recording begins Thursday. Got to have you. Call Sue for details. Ted

No airline ticket, no car rental slip, no receipts from hotels or restaurants, only the telegram, so Mara must not have gone, only Richard responding to this urgent message. Does the blank space indicate that she remained at home with Matt for only a few days or for several weeks, biding her time, being patient? Does it mean that she was busy and Richard was busy, exchanging no postcards of the Los Angeles skyline or of red double-decker buses? Does it mean they had no energy for one another?

Or is it as dangerous to read meaning into blank space as into a quiet telephone, an empty mailbox? After all, one has an obligation to assign significance—carefully.

Chapter 10

Mrs. D. frowned as she listened to Mara explain the ballot proposition. Mara had been helping her for several elections now, and Mrs. D. trusted her clear explanations and her honesty in marking Mrs. D.'s absentee ballot. Still, she wanted this young woman to appreciate that even the elderly have well-reasoned opinions.

"I think I'll have to vote 'No' on that one," she said firmly. "We'll cancel each other out, won't we?"

"I don't know," Mara shrugged. "On the one hand, jail sentences for pot smokers are way too stiff, but legalization may not be the answer either."

Mrs. D. broke off a small piece of pound cake, but most of it fell into her teacup. When she lifted the cup with a trembling hand, she didn't taste the solid flecks.

"I've read some of the arguments," Mrs. D. said proudly. She could picture how she'd sat with the magnifying glass, studying a page in the proposition booklet. "I agree with you about the prison sentences. They may indeed be far too long. But I just don't believe in legalizing a wrong. That's not the civilized way, you know, simply giving up like that. Now the one about parks—poke a 'Yes' on that one. I've always loved parks, especially if they're tended by a skilled gardener. Are we finished?" Abruptly, she lowered her voice. "I don't want my Lucy to hear, but she would say, 'Are we done?' I'm trying to teach her proper English usage. That's the least I can do, don't you think?"

Mara put down her pencil and smiled at Mrs. D.

"Does she appreciate it?"

Mrs. D.'s mouth made a small 'o' before she exclaimed, "I certainly hope so! I've loaned her most of my school books, and I listen very carefully so that I can catch her oral errors. Do you have to do much of that, dear, working where you do?"

Still smiling, Mara shook her head.

"I rarely try," she said. "How about these last three propositions? The ones on bonds?"

Mrs. D. leaned forward.

"Do you honestly know what a bond is?"

"A government loan. Something like that."

"Are they for libraries? Parks?"

Mara bent her head over the pamphlet, and Mrs. D. felt like touching that lovely long hair, shining in the sun, so different from her own gray wisps which stuck out like exposed wiring. Before Mara had come down for tea, Mrs. D. had asked Lucy to tuck her hair behind a comb decorated with fake jewels.

"Can't be done!" Lucy had laughed, turning Mrs. D. toward the mirror. "That hair won't be tucked! What it needs is a good shampoo. I wish you'd let me do you, or Clyde could drive us to that salon you used to like."

Mrs. D. had looked away from the mirror. That old lady isn't me, she had thought. She doesn't look anything like the person I am inside.

"Maybe someday," she had said.

Now, she admired Mara's hair, pulled back so neatly. That's the way a lady ought to look, she thought, and felt proud, as though Mara were somehow her doing.

"Did I catch you at a bad time?" Mrs. D. asked into the telephone. She could picture Mara sitting at her desk, turning the pages of a magazine or perhaps grading papers laid out below an expensive reading lamp, a china cup of steaming tea nearby to keep her alert.

"Oh—"

Goodness! Mrs. D. thought. What was that noise?

"Dear me," she exclaimed, "I must have—"

"No, no," Mara said, a bit breathless. "Matt was just grabbing for the—Mathew! Put that down! Excuse me—"

Mrs. D. could hear the receiver thud and a drawer bang. The kitchen, she thought. Not her den but standing by the kitchen desk.

Returning to the telephone, Mara said, "Sorry."

"I can hear him in the background. Does he want something?" Mrs. D. was pleased to be so observant.

"He always wants something," Mara answered.

She sounds disgruntled, Mrs. D. thought. Better get her mind off the child.

"I was just wondering if you could come down today."

"I'm afraid not," Mara said. "Richard's not home."

"He's at the studio?" Mrs. D. asked. I do enjoy saying that word, she thought, although I never can quite picture what a studio looks like. "Is he recording something?"

"Yes, a movie score, I think."

"I wanted to tell you about Wagner. I was listening to one of his operas this morning. He was wonderful, a genius. Thunderous, Nelson says, and I do agree. I think you're ready for Wagner."

She could hear Matt screaming "Mines! Mines!" but she persisted. It's better for children to see that parents have adult lives, she thought. Otherwise, they stay so self-centered.

"But you won't be down today?"

There was a sound of scuffling, then Mara's brief laughter.

"I really can't, Mrs. D."

"Do you think you could come tomorrow? I also have a letter I'd like to show you." Mrs. D. touched the envelope lightly.

"I don't know. I'll have to check with Richard and he won't be home until late."

"Nelson writes that he and Louise want me to have someone nearby I can call in case of an emergency. Could I rely on you?"

Is she listening? Mrs. D. wondered. All those noises.

"Mara?"

After a moment's hesitation, Mara asked, "What time do you think that would be?"

"I'm sure I don't know," Mrs. D. answered in amazement. "I'd try not to make it too late, but one can never tell about emergencies."

"Of course," Mara said, sounding distracted. "Whatever you need, Mrs. D." This will never do, Mrs. D. thought. This cannot count as human contact. I remember that's a problem when you have a baby—the absence of real conversation "Goodbye, dear," Mrs. D. said sternly.

Is it really that time again, Mrs. D. wondered. That Dewey man thought he would win, but Truman has fooled him and I'm glad. Never let on to Nelson, certainly not to Fritz, but I'm sure that Truman will do more for our country, more for the little people and my cats. They're such smart creatures. Really so intelligent. You can see it in their eyes. They know what I need. I've always said that. They can read my thoughts, I'm sure they can.

Wagner is so majestic. I hope Mara loves him the way I do. She needs quality in her life. It's hard when you have a baby, but quality must be continued. Love of the beautiful, the noble. People are so busy these days, rushing. Nelson, Louise. Fritz? No. Calm, steady. Never rattled, always quiet.

And causes. I make him take a stand. He gets so mad he makes up his mind.

More tea? No. I'll clean up later, or Lucy will do it tomorrow. I'm so tired, I can't even undress. Wrinkles. Hairpins. Pound cake…

Mrs. D. lay down on her rumpled blankets and was still for several moments, patterns of cats, trees, a skillet passing behind her lids. Suddenly, her eyes flew open and she turned onto her side, squinting into the shadows near the side door just a few feet from her bed, the door with a window above the handle. An arm! There it is on the other side of the glass! Is the door opening? Oh, my God!

Clutching her blanket, Mrs. D. screamed.

"Who is that? Get out of my house! How dare you—" and she screamed until she had to stop, breathless. The arm jerked away and the body was gone from the window.

Stumbling, Mrs. D. felt for the door lock, then the telephone. I have and he wants and I didn't lock…Dear God! I'm all alone!

In the darkness, she pushed Mara's number from memory.

"It's late, I know," she blurted out when Mara's sleepy voice answered, "but I just wanted—did you see—there was someone, a man—"

Clearing her throat, Mara asked, "Are you all right?"

"Yes, yes, but an arm…"

"Was there someone trying to get into your house? Mrs. D?"

"Yes…no…Your voice is so nice, dear. Just a familiar voice."

"Would you like Richard to come down? He could look around. Or we'll call the police."

Mrs. D. pulled the curtain across the window in the door. The fabric was thin and frayed, so the street light still shone through, but she felt safer.

"I'm fine now. Everything's all locked and your voice is so nice."

"Call Nelson in the morning."

"Oh, I don't want to bother him."

"But he wants to know how you're doing," Mara insisted.

"Fine, I'm doing fine. Besides, Fritz takes good care of me.   He was just napping, but he'll...I think I'll have French toast in the morning."

"Richard is coming right down, Mrs. D."

Richard. Milk.

"Do I have enough bread?" she asked. "One or two pieces, do you think?"

Company!   Mrs. D. reached up to her hair and wondered, for a brief moment, if she looked all right.

Scrapbook, page 12

This page is so full, so layered with notes and messages and a photograph, that the paper feels thick, ripping one hole and giving this page a special importance, as though it has been pawed over, added to, thought about.

First is a note card, carefully split down the crease so that the painting of a bouquet in soft pastels overlaps the half with handwriting, softens the inked letter and the message.

Mara, [the note reads]
Thank you so much for your call last night. As you know, Nelson and I have been increasingly worried about Gertrude. We will both be flying out on Wednesday to move her into a home. Please watch over her until then.
You have been most kind to Mother, and she, as well as we, deeply appreciates it.
Sincerely,
Louise Dunzler

But how can Mrs. D. move and the neighborhood remain the same? What if her house sells to active people who cannot be ignored or tolerated as an oddity but must be talked with, understood, taken into consideration? They may want to put on a new roof or enlarge the living room or build a fence. They may have annoying hobbies, such as tinkering with car engines. Besides, in a rest home, how can Mrs. D. play recordings of "La Bohème" and, in a quavering soprano, sing bits of everyone's songs? What becomes of her cats, the furnishings, the unfinished memoir pages?

Next to the stationery is an orange CITY COLLEGE telephone message.

M—[the message reads]
Monday, 1 p.m.
Mrs. D.—almost hysterical. Please call soon!—J
Then another—
Monday, 1:15 p.m.
M—
Mrs. D.—calmer. Told me about husband not liking Truman???—J
And below that a third—
Monday, 3 p.m.
M—
Mrs. D. is lonely. Are you leaving soon?—J

Does Mrs. D. know that her son is flying out—not to visit and discuss politics or her grandchildren's education—but instead to move her into a small room in a building crowded with other old people who do not care about spending time with her, listening to her, learning from her, people preoccupied with their own frailties? Is she panicked because her independence is abruptly going to end? Can she understand any of this, or is she simply, instinctively, clinging?

In the center of the bottom of the page is a piece of Mrs. D.'s stationery, creme-colored with a blue "D" swirled on the front. Inside is not her script, however, but Lucy's, jagged and tentative, as though her hand and her pen know that they should not be moving on this paper.

Dear Mara, [Lucy writes]

Thank you for taking my cats. I could not bear to abandon them. They are only one of the many reasons why I do not want to go.

Love,
Mrs. D. (Lucy)

PS Please do not come down.

Next is a receipt from SUNSET VETERINARY for administering vaccinations and neutering three cats, all of them male. But hadn't this been done already? Hadn't Mrs. D. insisted that her vet appreciated her frugality? Yet, here was Mara paying quite a large sum to alter the lives and habits of three creatures accustomed to creeping beneath porches in the dark of night, sniffing and leaping and curving their tails. Perhaps Mrs. D. deliberately had not neutered them, so that she could enjoy their nocturnal adventures while living a proper, sedate existence. Perhaps Mrs. D. had simply been confused.

On the left side of the page, offering a sudden richness of color, is a postcard, taped on all sides, so there must not be a message Mara wants to re-read occasionally. The picture is a photograph of a two-story, colonial house, white and gabled, shuttered and surrounded by trees. Connected to the house on one side is a white picket fence, through which a gate opens into a garden, lush with flowering bushes. Barely visible is the side of a royal blue gazebo. Lettering below the photograph identifies the building as THE MANOR: GRACIOUS, CHRISTIAN CARE.

So this is where Mrs. D. has moved. How elegant and refined. Surely something within her must appreciate that?

And in the center of this busy page, in the center of obvious activity and emotion, is a small—graph? diagram?—no, carefully lettered in white ink are the words SONOGRAM—M. LEEDS. This is a picture of a fetus— no, two fetuses!—still in the womb, lying with their tiny legs twisted into a heap. Carefully drawn arrows point to HEAD and THUMB—twice.

This is medical confirmation of what must have been an upheaval for Mara and Richard. This could not have been planned, but there sits the twins' first photograph, calmly surrounded by artifacts of Mrs. D.—not touching her, not touched by her.

Life begins. Life ends. Life is balanced.

Chapter 11

Hazel picked up her napkin, glanced at Richard, who hadn't reached for his yet, and quickly dropped the linen. I never have enjoyed restaurants, she thought. I don't feel comfortable and Mara seems restless. Maybe the babies inside are making her feel sick again, or maybe she doesn't like restaurants any better than I do. But it's Richard's birthday. He wanted to celebrate, and my visit just added to the reason. So here we sit, surrounded by linen and ferns. I'd better have a good time.

"Then what changed their mind, Richard?" Hazel made herself ask. Richard didn't often talk about his job, and she ought to be interested.

"When I said," he responded animatedly, "why not just record it here? We don't all have to fly across the country just because Scuds is based in New York. There are fewer of them. Pay them to come here!"

He reached out for Mara's hand. "Everyone said okay."

Mara smiled faintly and turned toward her grandmother.

"He's staying close to this frail woman," she smiled.

"You have your hands full, two babies inside and one out," Hazel responded. Privately, she wondered why on earth Mara had let this happen. One child was plenty, especially with a job.

"The doctor said today that I may start feeling better soon, or, on the other hand, I may not," Mara laughed. "Very encouraging. I'm glad I'm only working part-time and in the Study Skills Center. I couldn't have stood in front of classes or graded all those papers."

Mara took a long gulp from her water glass but, Hazel noticed, she didn't touch her wine.

"She also said that after six months, the risk is the same as for a normal pregnancy."

"What risk?" Hazel asked.

"The risk of the IUD causing problems. After six months, it won't."

"That's great!" Richard said, chewing with energy. "So you have one month left until you're out of the woods."

Hazel looked from one to the other.

"I don't understand. What's this IOU?"

"IUD, Grandma. Intra-uterine device. It's a little thing that floats around in the uterus and acts as a contraceptive."

"Only hers didn't," Richard laughed.

"You mean it's still in there?" Hazel demanded. "Some sharp thing near the babies?"

"Not sharp. But yes, it's somewhere in there. It won't cause deformities or anything, but it could cause an abortion."

"Abortion!": Hazel was stunned. "Shouldn't you be lying down? Taking medicine? Can't they get that thing out?"

Mara leaned away from the table, as though full after only a few bites of salad, and Hazel couldn't help staring at her belly. Floating in there were the babies in that picture, and hanging right next to them, evil and threatening, was a spiked instrument of death. How can we sit here, enjoying food, while death lurks nearby? How could we even think of celebrating when she has all that going on in her?

Hazel felt sick and she pushed away her food.

"Don't worry," Richard said, putting his arm around Hazel's thin shoulders. "Mara's being taken good care of, and she's not doing anything crazy. I've even canceled her skydiving lessons."

"Skydiving—!"

Mara laughed.

"He's only teasing, Grandma. Everything'll be fine, you'll see. Copacetic."

Hazel leaned back and frowned.

"Copacetic, remember?. Grandpa's word."

Doesn't describe me, Hazel thought, and not Al either, if he only knew. Or maybe he does.

The afternoon was smoggy and hot, the sort of day when Richard, hurrying off to an air conditioned studio, wanted Mara and Hazel to sit by the plastic wading pool, watching over Matt and sipping iced tea. Instead, they buckled themselves and the child into Mara's car for the drive to Pasadena and a visit with Mrs. D. Mara had promised, and Hazel had long been curious about her, having heard stories about how she'd voted or what she thought of the Great Society. Hazel had noticed that opera albums lined Mara's living room shelf, and that button number one in the car was a public radio station. She knew these interests reflected Mrs. D.

But it's more than just interests, Hazel thought. She's different, softer somehow, more womanly. Well, that may be marriage. Who knows?

Hardly admitted to herself let alone to her hosts, Hazel was relieved that Mrs. D. had moved. The woman took too much time. We old people have to be careful we're not a burden, and it sounded like Mrs. D. had been "put away" not a minute too soon, what with the pregnancy and Matt and all. I can't give her any of the credit, Hazel thought—she was going around the bend and probably didn't know the difference—but the timing was perfect.

Suddenly, Hazel decided that going around the bend wasn't such a bad idea. Eyes stinging from the thick air, she looked out the car window at freeway exits, heavy trucks and busy signs and thought, Maybe it isn't so bad not knowing what's going on. Maybe what I should hope for is the mind to go as the body crumbles. That way I wouldn't disgust myself.

By the time they reached the home, Matt was asleep and Hazel felt groggy, too. Only Mara seemed suddenly energetic as she strode toward the front door, pushing Matt in his stroller. A nurse's aide walking toward the elevator greeted Mara familiarly, and in a moment they all emerged directly across from Room 17.

The open door revealed floral wallpaper, a wicker bed stand next to a rumpled bed, and a small bookcase, empty except for a copy of the Bible and a framed photograph of Nelson, Louise and their two children. The windows were covered by curtains which matched the wallpaper and the whole room, Hazel thought, was an attempt to be gracious and homey, to make the patient and her visitors forget they were inside here instead of at home.

"Hi, there!" Mara cried out. A white-haired form was slumped in her wheelchair, forehead nearly touching the tray fixed across her lap.

"Look who's here!" the aide sang out as she pulled open a curtain. "Look who's come to visit you, Trudy!" Placing one hand on the form's shoulder, she gently pulled it to an upright position, and Mrs. D.'s eyes opened.

Hazel was startled. *This lump is not what I'd expected! Instead of a quick-witted, sharp-tongued, opinionated neighbor, perhaps ruling over the rest home from her bed, this is hardly a person. I'd known she had to be moved from her home, but surely she couldn't have been this bad off. Just what I'd heard: places like this make you get worse faster. That must be what happened.*

Mara bent close to Mrs. D.'s face.

"Hello!" she shouted. "I've brought two special people with me today!"

Gesturing toward Hazel, she pulled her gently toward the wheelchair, while she pushed back the stroller so that Mrs. D. could see Matt, now yawning and arching his back away from the stroller's canvas.

"I'm Hazel Severn, Mara's grandmother. Pleased to meet you," Hazel said, bending close. "Mara's mentioned you often."

"She's here on a visit." Mara said.

Mrs. D. blinked at Hazel, then Mara. I know that one, she felt. When my head clears, I'll know everyone.

The nurse straightened Mrs. D. in her chair and patted one shoulder.

"And look there, Trudy, your little Matt!" Leaning close to Mara, she barely lowered her voice. "She talks about him as though he was her own son."

Mrs. D. sat straighter and smiled as she saw the child, and Hazel frowned, suddenly protective of being the real relative.

"Baby!" Mrs. D. cried, and her voice was thin and tiny.

Mara lifted Matt from the stroller, exposing a damp circle where his back had been, and ruffled his hair.

"It's so hot outside," she said. "Lucky you have air conditioning, Mrs. D."

"Oh, it's always pleasant in here!" the nurse sang out. "Never too hot, never too cold. It's always just right, isn't it, Trudy?"

Hazel couldn't stand it. The wallpaper is too flowery, the nurse is too sickeningly cheerful, and Mara keeps waving Matt's arm and crying out in a baby talk voice, "Say hi, Matt! Say hi!" And there sits that lump. There's no life here! Dear God, Hazel thought, watching Mrs. D.'s face, listening for any sound from her, Dear God, may I never end up in a place like this. Let me die in my sleep or, like Phillip, step clean from the shower and bam! Life's done.

"It's a nice place, isn't it, Grandma?" Mara asked as they walked back to the car after staying only a few minutes more. "Grandma?"

"Well, now," was all Hazel could think of.

They say I'm not strong, Mrs. D. thought. They say my arms are weak, but sometimes they're not. Sometimes I can wheel myself, roll into the hall. I'm going to do that. I have to follow my baby. Where are they taking him? I can come out here and find Fritz and he'll find the baby. He'll find that woman. In the heat. Outside where it's hot. She said.

Here. The stairs. I don't need this thing. I can stand and walk. They won't let me, but I can. Curving stairs. My house. Fritz. Baby.

Where's Lucy? Down there? Holding my Nelson? Stairs. I've always been able…

Scrapbook, page 13

This blank page must commemorate a life now ended, as it did when Al died.

Scrapbook, page 14

Following is a page with a card and a photograph, squared off, side by side, as though there were no time to arrange them artistically, or as though artistry did not matter.

First the card. It is from Louise, and it has a printed message on the right side—THANK YOU FOR YOUR THOUGHTS DURING THIS TIME—and a note written neatly on the left:

Dear Mara, [Louise's note reads]

Thank you for giving Mother so many years of friendship and assistance. I'm sure you were as shocked by the call from the home as we were. Mother had always spoken of passing away in her sleep, but then, isn't that everyone's hope? We had a quiet service here and, as she had asked, her remains will lie next to my father's in Boston. They had always loved that city.

I don't know what's in the box. Mother asked me months ago to set it aside for you until she was gone. If the contents are peculiar, please understand. No one knows the world which Mother saw at the end.

Good luck with your babies.
Sincerely,
Louise Dunzler
And a PS written in another hand:
She loved you and you responded. The box doesn't matter. The love does.

Nelson

One lingers for a moment reading that card. It speaks well of two people, and it puts an end to an era, which must have caused Mara more than a little sorrow.

Next, the photograph. It is of Mara, dressed in a loosely fitting muumuu, legs crossed tightly at the ankles, Matt on her lap, lounging against the lump of her stomach. Next to her ankles is an empty cardboard box, a piece of pink tissue lying on the carpet.

In Matt's hands, held up to the camera, is a tape, with OPERA'S GREATEST ARIAS! lettered in black. Had Mara and Mrs. D. listened to that very tape, sitting in the warm sun and sipping from china cups while Mrs. D. hummed along?

And draped around Mara's throat, elegant against her hand which touches it almost apologetically, sparkles the pearl and emerald necklace. The necklace is thick and flashy, and it suits her even less than it did Mrs. D.—Mara is too young, the muumuu too casual. For years, since Fritz' death, where had this piece of ornate jewelry hidden? And had Mrs. D. ever told its story to Mara?

Probably not. But always, even near the end when people thought her a scattered old lady, Mrs. D. must have remembered the necklace. She must have hoped that, as a reminder of Mrs. D.'s—what? culture? values? life?— here, worn by a dear friend, was its proper home.

Carol Huebner

III

Pauline Halperin

Chapter 12

Reaching for what looked like a piece of lint, Pauline Halperin felt a sharp pain across her hip and sat up straight in her chair. She had forgotten: doctor's orders were not to touch the floor, and, since she'd volunteered at the hospital, she wanted to honor doctor's orders. Besides, she grimaced, it's easy to obey when it hurts if you don't.

Hip replacement surgery hadn't been too bad. The scar had healed nicely, and the physical therapist was complimentary about how fast she'd been up and around. She'd rented a walker, which she hated—at 72 she didn't feel old enough to be seen with one of those things—but at least she could manage at home now. Iona came in every morning and evening, and sometimes Iona's husband Tucker, and friends called to make sure Pauline was okay. She almost wished they didn't call so much, it was that hard to reach the phone, but she liked to talk, and the company was nice. If this had to happen at all, she thought, at least it had happened out here, where friends look out for each other, even if miles of desert do separate them.

Pauline stared out her open living room windows, feeling the warm breeze blow across her face. A double whammy, she thought. First a widow, then an invalid. She squeezed shut her eyes, as though not looking outside would help. But then, she saw Jerry cooking pancakes at the Sunday morning fundraisers for the Fire Station, or hollering during a baseball game on the radio, beer in one hand, pipe in the other. When she tried to block him, not see his lanky frame or wavy hair, she saw herself, collecting money at the breakfasts or, dressed in the pink jacket of a volunteer, wheeling patients down the hospital corridor. Suddenly, she saw herself sprawled in the parking lot, people hurrying toward her, arms waving. In the confusion, their voices changed from calling for help to yelling for a homerun—Jerry was suddenly there again, except he wasn't. She was loaded onto a stretcher and carried inside the hospital she had just left, and he never visited. She had to go through this alone.

Well, I'm doing it, she thought, and opened her eyes, not bothering to wipe her damp cheeks. Everyone worried about me, thought I'd ask for Anne to come get me, or cry on everyone's shoulder about how lonely I am or how sore or how afraid, living way out here. But I've been strong. Even my daughter would have to admit that. In fact, that may just be what most bothers her: widowed invalids should whimper. Otherwise, how's a daughter to know what to do?

Pauline thought of the guest bathroom and wondered if Iona had even looked in there. Here's Mara driving all the way out to see me, and I may have cobwebs over the toilet, she thought, but pulling herself up with her walker and going down the hall, not snagging the throw rugs or tripping on the small step, seemed like an awful lot of effort, so she sank back into the cushions and enjoyed the breeze.

Mara will understand. She and Richard have been coming out here since before they had kids, back when Jerry was alive. It had always been a sort of retreat for them, even when Anne couldn't be here. They'd loved the sound of wind in the cottonwood trees and staring at the clear views, not saying a word. They really love this place, Pauline thought, and she felt glad to still own it, to be able to share it with her friends—maybe her daughter's friends first, but her friends now.

Impulsively, Pauline dragged the walker close to pull herself up. It won't be spotless, she thought as she pushed herself down the hall, but certainly I can do *something*.

When Mara arrived, there was a fresh roll of toilet paper on the bar and on the counter a clean hand towel—smelling of sun and wind, Pauline had decided when she touched her face to the cloth.

"I couldn't remember," Pauline called out as Mara hurried toward the bathroom, "if you prefer the paper over or under."

"I assure you, it makes no difference as long as it's there," Mara laughed.

I'll be the gracious hostess, Pauline resolved. That way she can report back to Anne that—

"You look great, Pauline!" Mara said, sitting sideways on an upholstered chair and swinging her long legs over the arm. "Rested and even a little tan."

"Thank you! I feel stronger every day." She gestured toward the walker. "That's the only thing giving me away."

Mara smiled.

"We'll just call that your assistant," she said and they both laughed.

Mara swallowed from her glass of lemonade and set it carefully on the coffee table.

"Anne tells me you're planning to return to work."

Pauline nodded.

"I need it," she said, "and I love those people. They've been awfully good to me."

Mara will understand. Even if she doesn't agree, she'll try to see it my way.

"I'm a people-person, you know," Pauline continued. "Anne's not—at least, not as much as her mother—so it's hard for her to see how important that is to me. Contact. Human contact. Work doesn't drain me; it re-charges the old batteries!"

"When do you think—"

Pauline waved a hand.

"As soon as I can. I need it."

Reaching for the table, she grabbed her knitting needles, beginning to carefully count stitches.

"I have to hurry with this sweater," Pauline explained, "or I'll miss the holidays. Then I'd have to aim for Anne's birthday, which would mean making the sweater in a lighter weight of wool, or else she couldn't wear it until the winter, which isn't much of a birthday present in May!"

Pauline liked to talk and knit, as long as her companion wasn't bothered by her looking away and counting stitches.

"How's Richard?" she asked. "And the children? I was sorry they couldn't come along."

"Richard's busy with performances this weekend, so Rosie's caring for the kids."

"You told me about giving your housekeeper English lessons. How'd those work out?"

Mara shrugged, laughing.

"They weren't anything to add to my resumé. In fact, Rosie seems to learn faster if I *don't* try to teach her. So much for all my years of experience!"

She looks so sweet, so genuine, Pauline thought and felt suddenly protective.

"Don't be too hard on yourself," she said.

"But you'd think my work in a Skills Center would at least help me teach the poor woman how to run a washing machine," Mara insisted.

Pauline set her knitting on her lap.

"Maybe she's not mechanical," she cried. "I never was and I couldn't blame that on language."

Pauline smiled at the memory of soap frothing above the machine's lid, how Jerry had come running in, yelling, "For God's sakes, turn it off!" and she would have, if she could have remembered how.

"But she's good with the children?" Pauline asked, resuming her knitting. I want to know, she thought, and it's not meddling. We're just interested in one another, that's what it is.

Mara nodded.

"They adore her."

"It sounds to me," Pauline said, "like everything's going all right. Housekeeper, job, beautiful children." What a relief, she thought, and then laughed at herself. As though I had anything to do with it!

Mara watched her knit for a moment.

"And is Anne happy? She calls me occasionally, but it's mostly to talk about you, or the kids, or my job. I never make her talk about herself."

Pauline shook her head.

"She never has. Even when she was in college. It wasn't as though we lived far away. Just over in Downey and she was at UCLA, but we never heard from her. No calls, no cards. And Jerry's parents back in Illinois didn't get anything either. My mother started living with us then, and she used to complain that Anne was spoiled, but I thought, precious little time for being selfish, what with a sorority."

Pauline kept knitting, confident that she was understood by this comfortable friend.

"Years later I wondered about having my mother live with us," Pauline continued. "On the first look-see, it made sense. She'd just broken her hip, like me now, and she needed care. But I wonder if it was such a good idea. Has Anne ever said anything?"

Suddenly, Pauline felt guilty.

"You don't need to tell any secrets, you know," she interrupted herself. "You two are friends and she may say things to you which she'd never tell her mother. I don't want you to feel—"

"I would always tell you anything you needed to know," Mara assured her.

"You're a good friend to us both." Pauline leaned over the sweater, hiding her flushed face behind its patterned yarn. There are some subjects—like friendship—which always make me teary, and I don't know why, she thought. I should be too old for this.

Mara swung her legs onto the floor and leaned over.

"What do you need?"

"Nothing," Pauline said, pretending to be squinting at the floor. "I just thought I saw something, but who cares? Was it bothering you?"

"Not a bit."

Pauline chuckled.

"Then we'll just live and let live, I say."

Mara grinned at her.

"Being a good sport must help your recovery."

"I can live with limitations. Is that a virtue?"

"I don't know about virtuous," Mara answered, hanging her legs over the chair arm again, "but certainly healthy."

Pauline looked down at her hands, needles stopped.

"Tell my daughter I'm doing fine, will you?"

Mara nodded.

"I certainly will," she answered.

Leaning against two fat pillows, Pauline sat in bed, a tattered, leather-covered Bible open on her lap. The early morning sunlight, stretching in from over Goat Mountain, shone on the small type, and she struggled to keep her mind on what she was reading and not stare out the window. She knew that oleanders were blooming all over her garage and down the length of her house, thrusting their branches toward her windows. She could hear them scratching the glass in the afternoon wind, and she longed to just sit, enjoying the blossoms and the perfume of the sand.

But she had promised Jerry that she would read the Old Testament. It was something his aunt had made him do when he was a boy, and he had always regretted that Pauline had never had the same exposure to the beauty of the language, the grandeur of the ideas. One afternoon, almost beside herself with his diagnosis, she had made a deal.

"If it's what you want, of course I'll do it," she had murmured. "Maybe it will help pull us through."

"*You*," Jerry had corrected. "I'm not pulling through anything, but I'd like you to have that comfort."

Pauline had stared hard at her husband of fifty-one years.

"Maybe God will take pity on me," she'd said, but Jerry had shaken his head, one hand groping for hers.

"You don't need pity," he'd whispered. "Never did, never will."

Then came the caring for him, his death and the funeral and the visits from friends, then living in a daze before going back to volunteer work only a few days before she fell and broke her hip. During all that time, no Bible, she thought. Prayer, yes, lots of it, but she hadn't kept her promise about reading the Old Testament.

So now Pauline read deliberately, her lips moving:

"And God looked down upon the children of Israel, and God had respect unto them," she read aloud and looked up. "I wonder if God would have any respect for a poor lady who's only at—what? Exodus?"

Returning to the Bible, she had just begun to read about the angel appearing in a flame of fire when a face poked through the oleanders at her window, making her gasp, then laugh.

"Morning!" the cheery face called out. "Greeting the day, are we?"

"You startled me, Iona! Come on in."

The stout, flushed woman wearing baggy jeans let herself in the front door, pocketed her key, and marched into Pauline's bedroom.

"Well!" Iona boomed, "Did we have a good night?"

"We did, indeed," Pauline answered, closing the Bible gently and allowing herself to be swung around onto the edge of the bed.

"In this big old king-sized monstrosity?"

Standing stiffly, Pauline steadied herself on the walker handles and looked over her shoulder.

"That's a beautiful bed, Iona."

"Too high and too wide," Iona bellowed.

"Jerry loved it," Pauline insisted. "He was so tall, that was the only place he could really be comfortable."

Iona gripped one elbow and pulled Pauline toward the bathroom, but she held back.

"I can do all right. Really," Pauline protested, but Iona had already slammed the door behind both of them, the top of her underpants showing as she bent over the toilet to adjust the seat and tug at the toilet paper.

"You do this?" she cried. "The loose end should come over the top!"

"Well," Pauline said, resigned to assistance, "that's as may be," and she began to loosen her robe.

Scrapbook, page 15

SMALL WORLD PET STORE prints colorful receipts, with pink cats and blue dogs twisting around the edges. Scrawled in the middle is the amount "$35" and the tiny printing "C Span." The longer receipt is much more revealing: it lists in computer type a variety of dog products, everything from a food dish to flea powder, the total of $42.83 being charged to VISA. The store's address is Los Angeles, so this purchase—of a cocker spaniel?—must be by Mara and Richard.

No photograph accompanies these receipts, but something better does: a child's drawing of a hairy mound of black and white with two enormous black dots as eyes and a red tongue arcing toward a smiling sun. Behind the mound are five stick figures, one tall, the next shorter with a triangle skirt, the next with a long arm touching the triangle, and the last two smaller than the dogs' eyes. Dominating the three visible faces are grins from ear to ear. The dog's tail fattens the M of the signature: MATT the red crayon spells, each letter falling closer to the edge of the paper.

No close study is needed to decide that the stick figures are happy to be standing in the sun with their nice dog, and the dog is happy to be with them.

Below the drawing is a small card with the illustration of a puppy on the front, dancing around a flowered bush. Inside is a message in Pauline's large handwriting:

Dear Friends, [Pauline writes]

Your news was wonderful. I love dogs and I miss my doxy very much, so I just may follow suit. Something small I could do with easily. Humid out here so the days go slowly with not much accomplished. Hip is doing great. I should go back to volunteer work next month.

Love to all and especially to Patches—
Pauline

Next to that is glued a small bookmark, beige with a brown cross above a lush pasture scene and lettering in the center: "We came unto the land and surely it floweth with milk and honey and this is the fruit of it." Numbers 13.

The bookmark could have fit inside Pauline's card. Did it? Perhaps the quote from Numbers was her way of telling Mara how far she had progressed in reading the Old Testament. Perhaps it was her way of trying to influence, to set an example. (If that is so, then Pauline would not be happy to see it mounted here instead of marking a Bible.)

Or perhaps Mara bought it herself, smiling at the notion of the abundant fruit which she and Richard had produced. Too much milk and honey, she might think, but such delicious fruit, and so precious to us. Exhausting but precious.

Bookmarks are odd things: should they be read and appreciated for themselves or are they inconsequential scraps to mark more important words?

Chapter 13

"You don't like to cook, do you?" Shirley asked. She sat at Pauline's dining room table, her chin resting in a hand while she watched Pauline move from freezer to counter.

Pauline turned to face her, an empty chicken pie box in her hand, the open flap coated with ice.

"Not much. But my cooking was okay with Jerry. He used to call it 'solid American'—you know, meatloaf and potatoes. Now that I'm alone, I've gotten to like these frozen things. Quick and easy, that's my style."

She looks so—oh, offended, sort of, Pauline thought.

"You're a wonderful cook, Shirley," Pauline said, reassuringly. "I know your chicken pies would be lots better than—" she squinted at the box she was dropping into the trash— "Lady Lee."

Shirley smiled as she nodded.

"Pete's often said that I could cook for a living," she said. "Make meals for shut-ins and deliver them, you know? By the way, I have the new *Sunset*. It's got a yummy-sounding recipe for lamb stew baked right in the pumpkin. You ever cook from recipes?"

Pauline shook her head.

"Not much any more," she said, but she walked quickly out of Shirley's view, busying herself at the sink, because truly, she thought, there'd never been a time when I'd enjoyed puttering around the stove, and I've always felt bad about that. Women of my generation like to cook. That's how they show love and caring for their families. But what did I do? I told stories, mostly about people who worked at the office or some of our crazy clients. I brought home a paycheck and I talked. Did that show Anne how much I loved her? Could I have made a happier home by serving lamb stew in a pumpkin?

"Your daughter's handy in the kitchen, though," Shirley said, sounding puzzled.

"My mother lived with us, and Anne helped her cook," Pauline explained. "Mama would be proud, seeing her granddaughter create a knockout dinner from scraps—strange-looking food, Jerry always said, but tasty. "Now my head has pictures of two people—my mother and my husband—and I don't want to think about either one of them. If I'm going to do okay, I can't dwell on those two people.

"Just to show how little I cook," she said cheerfully, "I don't even remember what's in those." She waved toward four tin canisters on the counter. "Anne dusted them, arranged them like that, but I don't think even she could pry the lids off. Who knows?" Pauline cried, "boll weevils might crawl out!"

Shirley didn't smile.

"Your kitchen needs a good cleaning," she mumbled, then looked at her watch. "I've got time. Want me to have a go?"

Pauline slapped down a plate holding the chicken pie, pushed the pie back into the center and gestured.

"Relax," she said. "I may be setting before you life and good or death and evil—that's what it says in Deuteronomy."

"I don't think Moses was referring to pot pies, Pauline," Shirley said.

"We'll never know, will we?" Pauline asked and hurried off for another fork.

"Mother, you shouldn't be working," Anne protested. "Your body needs more time to recuperate."

Holding the phone with her shoulder, Pauline slid her bookmark into the Bible and shut it firmly. She was up to Joshua now and careful about marking her place.

"Six hours a week isn't such a long time, Anne, and only two at one stretch. I like being back. The nurses and doctors are terrific. They think I'm doing great, by the way."

"They'd probably think you were doing even greater if you doubled your hours. How can you be sure they don't just need you working?"

Pauline liked the sound of that.

"I hope they do," she said. "By the way, Russell says hi. He still remembers you from our fiftieth anniversary party."

Unbidden, a clear picture appeared—of the club ballroom, balloons and streamers, tables of food and champagne, and the enormous poster Anne had made of Pauline and Jerry's wedding photo. There it hung above the conversations and the dancing, two naive, young faces grinning down on the now silver hair of their friends. "Russell married another orderly, a pretty young woman named Betty or Barbara," Pauline said quickly. "They make such a nice couple and hard-working, both of them—"

"—Mother," Anne's voice cut in, "listen to me. I'm telling you I'm concerned. Give me the number of the hospital."

Startled, Pauline asked, "Whyever?"

"So I can call the director of volunteers and get a handle on all this. You have to appreciate my position. I'm thousands of miles away, you're alone, and you're making decisions without consulting me. I get worried."

"I *am* seventy-two years old, Anne. After that many years I should know what's best for me." I never sound like this, Pauline thought, unless I'm talking with my daughter. What is it about her that brings this out in me?

"But you've never been seventy-two before, Mother, or widowed or recovering from surgery, so this is new territory for both of us. I'm simply worried. Could I have the number, please?"

Pauline recited it from memory, she had used it so often: calling the volunteer office to confirm her hours, or calling a doctor for herself or, before that, for Jerry. She liked the place. It was a group of caring people, and she liked to think they cared about her for more than professional reasons. If her daughter called, what would they tell her? And might they cancel Pauline's hours just to avoid any more calls like that?

"Have you heard from Mara lately?" Anne's tone was lighter now. "I owe her so many letters, it's ridiculous. Every time she sends more pictures with a note, no matter how short it is, I feel guilty."

Pauline made herself respond affectionately.

"Same with me. Her kids look darling. Well, what would you expect, such handsome parents." Pauline hesitated and then gambled. "Just as yours would be, you and Fred being a handsome couple."

"I know. Too bad the world will miss the sight of our kids."

So she hasn't changed her mind, Pauline thought. That gives me such pain, as though she'd slapped my face or yelled at me that I wasn't a great mother myself. Pauline shook her head and began, unconsciously, to finger the Bible.

"I'm up to Joshua," she announced.

"Oh."

"The language makes for slow-going, but I'm enjoying it."

"That's good."

She doesn't care, Pauline thought. She's never really taken to religion. I bet she hasn't been inside a church since she got married. Well, I won't say anything. I'll just keep this to myself, so we don't have another topic to argue about. I won't 'move my tongue' against my child.

Pauline smiled to herself. If only Jerry could hear me quoting from the Bible. What a kick.

"I don't know why I let you talk me into this!" Iona screamed from the edge of the pool. "I hate water!"

Pauline waved but said nothing so that she could continue her lap, holding onto the foam kickboard and moving her legs as steadily as possible. The instructor was looking from Iona to her, as though worried that Pauline's guest might spoil her progress, and Pauline wanted to show that she was still concentrating.

The water feels cool, she thought, not too cold because of all the folks with arthritis, but just refreshing enough that I'm glad I made the effort to come, even is it did mean putting on a bathing suit—*that 's* the part I hate, not the pool itself. Seeing myself in the dressing room mirror is always a disappointment, no matter how I talk to cover my feelings: lumpy, is how I'd describe my body, lumpy and formless. What has become of the trim waist, the high breasts, the hips almost too narrow for childbirth? How did that shape dissolve into this mound of dough? I don't even have the excuse of many children.

"How many laps, Pauline?" the instructor called, kneeling at the end of the pool.

Pauline slapped the kickboard onto the cement.

"Fifteen," she answered, shaking water from her permed hair while she held the edge, "and that's enough for today, Sue."

"Don't you feel great?" Sue cried cheerfully. "Just knowing you got some exercise?"

Hand over hand, Pauline began moving toward the ladder, Iona behind her.

"I don't know about my friend," called Iona up to Sue, "but I'm just glad to be alive."

In the locker, Pauline avoided looking at the mirror until she was fully dressed in her pants and loose blouse.

"Have you ever read the Book of Ruth?" she asked Iona, leaning close to the mirror to put on her lipstick.

"I told you once and a thousand times," Iona laughed., grabbing her purse and rolled up towel, "I never read the Old book, only some of the New. Ask me about Matthew."

Pauline shook her head.

"I'm not there yet. But the Book of Ruth ends with a slew of begats. Eight, I counted, all the way down to David."

"And he stopped the begetting?"

Pauline chuckled.

"I imagine there was more."

Together they walked down the hall toward Iona's old truck, shimmering with waves of desert heat.

"Today I couldn't help thinking about begetting. I had only the one child, so there's no excuse for this body."

"And you don't eat anything," Iona said, turning the key in the ignition.

"Of course, I eat *some*thing, Iona."

Iona punched on her blinker.

"Still," she said, "gravity sets in somewheres along the way and begins to pull us down into the grave. That's what I think."

Pauline stared out the car window, and Iona leaned over the steering wheel to see her face.

"You're not getting religious on me now, are you?" Iona asked.

Pauline looked back at her.

"Because like I told you once before, I'm not a believer. Haven't been my whole life. But I've done pretty good by people, I think. Good without benefit of clergy, that's me." Iona laughed again, a hearty explosion of sound and spittle.

"So you've never gone to church?"

"Never. That bother you?"

"No, but I think it's too bad," Pauline said.

"You Christians always feel sorry for us non-believers, as though we're losing out. I don't want you to go preaching at me, Pauline. If I feel the need, I'll let you know. Until then, keep the Bible reading to yourself, if you don't mind my saying so."

Pauline suddenly felt as though glass encased her, trapped her away from sharing with anyone, like the bubble the Pope rode around in. I wish I'd begun reading the Old Testament when I could still talk to Jerry, she thought. He would have appreciated my ideas, and he would have liked seeing the Bible open on the table or next to the bed. He would have made me feel good about that. As it was, Anne is—terse, Mara would say, and the only person I spend regular time with doesn't want me to talk about religion.

When they reached Pauline's house, Iona turned to swing her legs out the door.

"Thanks for driving, Iona," Pauline said, touching Iona's arm to stop her. "You get on back to Tucker."

Iona frowned.

"But I want to see that you eat some of that salad and casserole I made."

"I will, really. It looks delicious."

"But that casserole is heavy."

Pauline patted her arm.

"I'll be fine, Iona. And thanks."

Pauline held herself extra-steady as she walked past the oleander bushes near the front door, knowing that Iona was watching for any bobble as an excuse to dart head of her into the kitchen. I'm hardly a queen there, she thought, but it *is* mine.

Scrapbook, page 16

At the top of this page are two photos with a pink index card taped between them. The left photo is of Pauline sitting in a metal lawn chair, a glass of iced tea on the table beside her. She is wearing a floppy hat, broad-brimmed and bright yellow, below which her sunglasses are barely visible, but her lips are spread in a grin nearly as wide as her hat. Over one shoulder, hanging from a branch of a cottonwood tree, is a plastic hummingbird feeder with a tiny bird at one red spout, its brilliant blues and greens glinting for the camera.

The other photo is of a complete mess, the kind of mess only children can make. On a concrete, outdoor step melted crayons form a puddle over their flattened box and a firetruck lies on its side, oozing something thick and purple. The screen door is missing its top hinge, and chocolate brown coats the handle. A waxy, black line wiggles down the wire and then dashes across the screen, widening as it reaches the other side. Woven through the wire mesh are lavender petals and dark green leaves, probably from the now-bare rose stalk in a pot near the step. Sticking straight up through the gap at the bottom of the screen is a doll's leg: long and skinny, it is tipped by a black high-heeled shoe which points toward the door. Popsicle sticks pattern the step—one is caught in the melted crayons—and flies dot a plate of cookies.

Behind the screen stand three children, the tallest smiling happily, enjoying having a camera freeze this memento of a wonderful afternoon, the other two smaller, wide-eyed, not quite sure why they have been called to the door.

On the pink card between the two photos is printed in Mara's writing, PERHAPS THE SAME DAY—DEFINITELY A DIFFERENT POINT IN LIFE.

Below is a child's drawing on a torn sheet of lined paper: two rounded figures given colorful clothes and happy smiles, the man holding a clarinet below ragged half notes which are floating into the sunny sky. MATT is scrawled across the bottom, followed by I LOVE MOMMY AND DADDY.

This is a happy page, capturing color and pleasures and satisfaction, not including the clean-up of the stair.

Chapter 14

Pauline leaned back in the heavily upholstered chair and smiled at Richard.

"I can't get over this hotel!" she said. "It's almost more luxury than I can handle."

Richard passed her the dinner rolls in their dark basket.

"Pretend you live like this all the time," he whispered. "They don't ever need to know the truth."

Mara turned from one of the two high chairs, its tray covered by plastic toys.

"What are you two whispering about?" but Richard put his finger to his lips, winked at Pauline and shook his head.

Delighted to feel part of a group, Pauline leaned across the table toward Hazel.

"Isn't this wonderful? The hotel is so beautiful and you must love seeing Mara and the darling babies. Imagine being able to just ring them up on a house phone!"

She smiled, her cheeks made redder by the wine, but Hazel sat stiffly and said nothing. This was more activity than she normally saw at even the busiest Sunday School class: waiters, arms lined with plates, Ken and Marika pounding toys on their high chair trays, Matt next to her leaning so far off his booster seat that she frequently extended a palm to keep him from falling, plastic bags of Cheerios, coloring books and crayons dumped around her salad plate. Adding family to my vacation maybe wasn't such a good idea, she thought. I could have stayed home. I love Mara, but I could have told her to just send pictures.

Feeling rebuffed by Hazel's silence, Pauline turned toward Richard.

"It's too bad you couldn't stay longer out here. You could come up to the house and relax for a few days. Tall drinks under the trees—what were those drinks Anne made that time you were all there?"

"Wine coolers," Richard answered. "A little weak, but delicious. That was a special weekend, Pauline. You waited on us hand and foot while we did nothing but talk. Of course, that was B.C."

"Before Children," Mara laughed.

Matt toppled from his booster and howled, stopping abruptly when Richard scooped him up and rubbed his bare knee. Uninterested in their older brother, the twins continued pounding toys on Cheerios, smashing the cereal circles to a powder.

Untroubled by the din, Pauline said, "Anne won't be coming out at Christmas. Fred's parents want them to go there, so I won't be seeing them for awhile. Where are you going for the holidays, Hazel?"

Hazel nearly jumped, so hard was she trying to detach herself from the group.

"Stay home, by myself." And love it. Have I become so—irascible? Nine letters, too long for Scrabble but a possibility in a puzzle.

Pauline set down her fork carefully. She knew she hadn't talked this out with Anne, and yet, here they were, Richard and Mara, so much like her own. The moment seemed right.

"After the holidays, I think I'll list the house," she announced.

Mara stopped distracting Ken with a carrot stick, and Richard straightened behind Matt's chair. Hazel looked around the table and realized that something significant had been said.

"List' as in move?" Richard asked.

Pauline nodded.

"Anne says the High Desert is changing, and she's right. When Jerry and I bought our place, it was a quiet retirement area. The worst we saw were a few motorcycle gangs. But now people drive up my road at night, and the hospital is full of young girls who are overdosed. The town is trying to attract families from the Marine base: big shopping centers, banks, car dealers. Even a porno theater. That's what really bothered Anne, the last time she came out. You young liberals, not tolerating pornography," she smiled, but Mara leaned forward in alarm.

"Where would you go?"

Pauline swallowed. Where indeed? she thought. Just what I've been wondering.

"I mean, I can't imagine your not being on the desert. Would you move down here to Palm Springs?"

Pauline shook her head.

"I can't afford it, and I don't fit. These are moneyed people, you know, and I work at a community hospital, eat at the volunteer fire department. Oh, by the way, I went to a game at their baseball diamond, the one Jerry set up. The team captain is a little girl who has long blond hair, and she can really hit the ball. They're going to wash cars to raise money for bleachers, maybe a dugout."

Richard sat down again.

"Where to, Pauline?"

Hazel was glad someone had returned the woman to her topic. That's the trouble with talking: you can drift away from the subject and then the air is just full of sound.

"Perhaps I'll join Anne in Tennessee."

"Tennessee?" Mara cried. "All the way back there?"

"Unless my brother persuades me to go to Indiana. He's never thought I had much of a brain. It all went to him, which he thinks is only right, because he's the man. He likes me to apologize all the time, Mara. I thought of him when I was reading the Book of Samuel and the servant pleads with the king not to 'impute iniquity'—what a good phrase. That's what Ray does—'impute iniquity' on me."

"Then why would you go there?" Mara asked.

"Family. I'd be going back to my birthplace as opposed to interfering in my daughter's life. Perhaps if she had children…But that's not going to happen. I don't know. It's a decision."

The table was quiet. The twins had fallen asleep, cheeks pressed against the crumbs on their trays, and Matt was absorbed in watching a guitarist prepare to sing. The singer was dressed in black and, leaning into the microphone, he half-shut his eyes:

> I don't want you, baby,
> Unless you want me, too.

His voice was a syrup, thickly coating their conversation, slowing it to a halt, while he stroked the strings of his guitar softly, sensually:

> I've never needed anyone,
> As much as I need you.
> But it don't matter, baby,
> If you don't want me, too.

Absently, Hazel reached out and touched Matt's hair, tracing the curl at his neck.

"Old age is no fun, is it, Hazel?" Pauline asked quietly, as though everyone were asleep but them. "A friend once said that after forty there's no good news. He was only half joking.":

Hazel pulled her fingers free of Matt's hair and looked carefully at this woman, this friend of Mara's. She's a nice lady, Hazel thought, if a little chatty.

"It'll be fine," Hazel said. "However you decide, you'll make the best of it." Hazel wondered how she knew that, but there was no time to pull back the words and think about them.

"Of course you're right," Pauline smiled, and the two of them watched the singer.

"Your face looks puffy, Mara, as though you've been crying," Hazel said, after the waiter had taken their breakfast order.

Mara looked down.

"Intimations of mortality."

"What?"

"Pauline's moving away and you're 85. This may be the last time—we're all together."

What she means, Hazel thought, is that this may be the only time before Pauline and I die.

"We're both old," Hazel said, "so you may be right."

Reaching out for Mara's hand, Hazel added quietly, "I've been through this before, being left behind. Death hurts the living. There's no getting around that."

Mara looked up.

"But you're both important to me. How can I say goodbye tomorrow?"

The waiter, glancing nervously at Mara, set down two bowls of oatmeal and hurried away.

"As you always have," Hazel said, "bravely." Squeezing Mara's hand, she added in a more cheerful voice, "Now, let's eat until we have eaten to our entire sanctification!"

"Grandpa's words," Mara said.

"How did it end?" Hazel demanded.

"If I should eat any more, I should be flippis floppis."

"Excellent," Hazel said. "I'm glad you remember."

Pauline was first to leave. Iona and Tucker pulled their old truck into the hotel's parking lot before lunch, honking and waving, and Iona bounded out of the driver's seat.

"Hello there!" she cried to the group standing near Mara's car. "Let's get a move on, Pauline, before the heat gets horrible. No air conditioning in this old jalopy, you know."

Grabbing Pauline's bag, she pushed her toward Tucker and the open car. Pauline barely had time to kiss everyone and wave before disappearing into the back seat. She twisted around to watch them through the gun rack: Mara swung her arms broadly, as though stopping a train, Richard stood still, the children's fingers folded up and down, and Hazel, after a brief flick of the wrist, turned back to Mara's car.

"The heat down here is lots worse than at home," Iona called over her shoulder. After a pause, she said, "Didn't mean to rush you."

Pauline clicked shut her set belt and her lips, deciding not to complain. I should be glad for friends, she thought, people who'll take care of me. For a moment she remembered the Children of Israel, but quickly she put aside the comparison.

Hazel watched the dusty car turn at the palm tree and thought, Pauline has friends. It's not that I'm jealous. After all, I could have more, but I didn't want any after Al. He was it, the best. Not long after I lost him, Rose passed on. Then Phillip. That's what old age requires, keeping track of deaths. I could list 'Deaths' in the anniversary section of my address book. Give me something to write there.

And then Mara and her family were gone. Hazel didn't want it to be a lingering departure—she hated those—so she simply hugged everyone quickly and slammed their doors.

Absent-mindedly touching what remained of her ear, she mumbled, "Well, now." and walked toward the hotel's entrance, lonely in the sudden quiet.

Scrapbook, page 17

Glued across the top of this page is an article too short for the large photograph which accompanies it: Hazel at her desk, small but stiff in her straight-backed chair, typewriter filling the blotter. She is not smiling, just staring at the white paper in front of her, her glasses chain somehow making her look official, business-like.

The article says she is writing another letter to the mayor, complaining about the fifth dangerous intersection she has identified and asking that the city erect stop signs. "Each intersection takes several letters, spaced a few days apart," she is quoted. "I didn't ask anybody to help me. I'm not part of a group, only one old lady who wants to see something fixed." The newspaper states that this one lady just may accomplish what a citizens action group could not: the signs had been approved and would be in place by week's end.

When asked if she'll throw a party, Hazel says no. She's too busy working on her next cause: a homeless shelter sponsored by local churches. "You're indefatigable," the interviewer says. "To which Hazel Severn replied, 'Nice word, but too long for much use."

Below the article is a cluster of ticket stubs: the LA Philharmonic, the Long Beach Symphony and one, set apart, to hear Placido Domingo. Only one stub for each event. Did Mara's companion keep the ticket, or did Mara go alone? This question is answered by a slip of paper pasted next to the tickets, paper torn from larger, nice-quality stationery. The handwriting is Loreen's.

"Let me say this: [Loreen writes] *I'm glad Domingo was wonderful, but your father would have never approved of your attending events without your husband. Attending*

with gay men—well, I can't begin to think what he'd say about that. The fact that they're friends of your husband is almost worse."

That fragment of a letter tells us about Loreen and Phillip, about Richard and Mara. Something so brief can tell a lot when it is about values.

On the bottom of the page, glued so that it cannot be turned over, is a professionally printed flyer, a narrow rectangle picturing a long house and in the white space next to it, the words: FOR SALE! $95,000 STEAL! Drawn below those words in black ink is a frowning face and sad eyes. This picture is Pauline's home; this must be her realtor's announcement. The face, probably drawn by Mara, tells her feelings about Pauline's move, as the tickets and letter fragment above tell her feelings about cultural events, gays, her parents' opinion.

So many values crowded onto one page.

Chapter 15

How did I come to be here? Pauline marveled, balancing a plate of French bread and apple slices while she took a piece of cheese. Looking around her, she saw half a dozen laughing young men and women, younger than her Anne. They seem glad I'm here, she thought. That's surprising but very nice.

Not twenty minutes ago, she had been on the road, rushing to get here with her dog shaking beside her in the car, one paw stretching slightly above the seat. The driver of an oncoming pickup truck had hollered out his window at her, jabbing his middle finger into the air. Shrinking in her seat, she had been ashamed for the young man. I didn't deserve it, she had thought. I couldn't have been *that* close to the line.

Collecting herself, she had said in as comforting a voice as possible, "It's okay, Sniffy. We'll be there soon."

The dog had darted a look up at her but quickly pressed further into the cushions. She'd known that his shakes were not the result of her driving but of his fear at being hurt, and her foot had pressed the gas a little harder. Mara often called these roads 'roller coasters,' she thought, because they had such low dips and steep rises. If only I could be driving a straight, level freeway. Turning off the radio, she had concentrated on steering and speed.

The animal hospital was a low, white stucco building on a side road off the main highway, its parking lot dirt to the edge of the building. Boarding kennels and some open-air runs ringed the back of the building. I like coming here, Pauline had realized. I like the sounds of dogs, the practicality of the staff. I even like the smells—shampoo, alcohol, kibble and urine all mixed together. It's a whole lot different from my hospital. Even the staff's jeans, torn shirts and spotted white coats reassure everyone that dirt's okay here, and fear, too. In a people hospital, Pauline thought, dirt was banished and fear was hidden.

The vet had walked casually into the front room where Pauline was waiting alone on the long sofa. Pauline was always startled by Dr. Macy's pretty gold earrings: so delicate next to her thick glasses and too shiny for her scruffy clothes and heavy shoes.

"You know what it was?" the young woman had asked, seating herself next to Pauline. "A cactus nettle, way down into the flesh, and then two burrs in the pad of his foot. He must have been really hunting around outside."

"Oh, he loves the yard," Pauline had laughed with relief. "He sniffs around out there by the hour—well, there you have his name! So can I take him home?" Pauline had begun to stand.

The vet had put out a hand, palm down.

"Stay!" she'd commanded and they'd both laughed. "Sorry. I forget I'm working with people, too. Sniffy's sleeping off the anesthetic for another half hour or so. Meanwhile, you want something to eat? Kelly brought a bunch of goodies for lunch."

"You're welcome to join us, Mrs. Halperin!" called out the slender girl with the long perm. She was already arranging a buffet behind the counter. "Not a gourmet feast, but it beats driving in to town."

So here I sit, Pauline thought, having this delicious picnic around the reception desk, watching—kids, she thought of them—amuse each other, flirt a bit. And it's so good to see how friendly Barbara Macy is with her staff, natural, easy-going. Pauline could tell that the kids liked their boss a lot.

"I had a cat once," Kelly was saying to her, "who used to start purring when I read aloud. 'Course, it wasn't the Bible, like you're doing. Just anatomy, biology, science textbooks, stuff like that. But she liked the sound of my voice, I guess, and it sure beat studying in silence."

"Try not studying at all!" a young man said. Someone had used his name, but Pauline had forgotten it. All she knew was, she liked his curly hair.

"No study, no jobbie," Kelly said, reaching for a pickle. "You don't need to work?"

Curly Hair winked at Pauline.

"Is it required?"

Ignoring him, Kelly turned back toward Pauline.

"So tell me, how long have you lived out here?"

"And why on earth would you?" Curly Hair interrupted.

Pauline smiled at both of them. Such nice young people!

"Ten years, but I've had my house on the market for awhile. I was thinking of joining my daughter in Tennessee or else my brother, but nothing much is selling, I guess."

"You have no family around here?" Barbara asked.

"Only friends, and I'll miss them. But I have to admit, I get afraid living alone." Pauline felt better to see Barbara nod sympathetically.

"Why the choice?" she asked.

Pauline explained about her brother and her daughter, in greater detail than she would have except that they all looked so interested and asked such good questions. An informal vote sided unanimously with moving to Tennessee. It amused Pauline how easily they ruled out her brother. Curly Hair called the advantages of living near him "miserable comforters."

"That's from the Bible," he explained in a mocking tone, "in case you poor heathens didn't recognize it as Job."

Everyone hooted.

"*I'm* not a heathen," Pauline said as the comments died down, "but I haven't gotten to Job yet."

"Where are you?" he asked.

"Chronicles. But to tell the truth, I'm not enjoying it much. Even Sniffy wants out, and he's always been such a loyal listener."

Curly Hair jumped to his feet, spread out his arms and legs, and pinched shut his eyes.

"Hear me, brothers and sisters!" he cried, and Pauline laughed but leaned forward, eager for his imitation of a rousing preacher. "Know that Chronicles may be boring, yes! Both I and II. And then comes Ezra and Nehemiah and—Amen, brother!—Esther! Are they gripping? Will you rock and moan? No, sisters! But what is next? Tell me, what comes after Esther?"

Everyone sat grinning, but no one spoke.

"The Book of *Job*! Amen! The Book of Job! And after that? The Psalms! Then Proverbs! Yea, in those books the Bible is *rich*, brothers and sisters, rich and full of wisdom. Then you shall cry out! The truth shall make you free!"

Kelly poked his leg, someone else threatened to toss soda in his face, and Curly Hair collapsed, flushed but obviously proud of himself. Everyone laughed and talked at once, pounding his knee, punching his shoulders, questioning how he remembered all that, teasing him about getting high marks in Sunday School. In the midst of the laughter, Pauline realized that he had succeeded in making her excited about what was coming. In fact, she resolved as she cleaned up, I just may skip up to Job right now.

In a few moments they were all back at work and she was on the road, a limp dog lying next to her. Pulling her car into the garage, she scraped the bumper against the old freezer and surprised herself. I'm wearing my glasses, she thought as she inspected the marks, and it's not dark, so how did that happen? But Sniffy needed her attention, so she quickly forgot about her driving.

"No, I wasn't asleep," Pauline assured the caller, "only resting. I had a big day yesterday, taking Sniffy to the vet, and then I bent over to check her paw, which I forgot I can't do too easily yet. I can do housework, change my bed, but I can't lean down to the floor. That's the darndest thing, Mara."

"Frailty. One day we have to accept it into our lives."

"Isn't that the truth?" How can she be so young but so wise? Pauline wondered. "My arthritis has been bad lately—it's this weather—so I had to stop that muffler I was knitting Fred. Iona even cooked me dinner several times last week. If I could go to the pool, I'd probably feel better, but it's just too much trouble."

"Small children are like frailty, Pauline: they end spontaneity." Mara laughed. "Sometimes Richard and I have a whole afternoon where we could all go off to the park or the beach, but by the time we've packed everything, we're too tired to enjoy ourselves."

The two women chuckled together.

"You know what else?" Mara continued. "I've had to learn to ask for help. Suddenly, this capable woman can't manage without all sorts of assistance, and that hurts. I've even heard myself telling colleagues that I need to hire a grader—all because of the kids!"

"Oh, I know just what you mean! I tried to talk to Iona about it the other day, but I never could find the words, and I certainly wouldn't want to hurt her feelings, bless her heart. What would I do without her? But that's just the point: I get tired of needing her! I want a vacation from all that."

"A vacation from dependency."

"Exactly." It's more than understanding, Pauline thought. We share. Why can't one's own children do that? I guess just because they *are* our children. Anne's so used to fussing at a parent, she can't see the opponent fading, but there it is. Pauline sighed.

Changing the subject, she asked, "How's Hazel?"

"She just had her 86th birthday," Mara answered. "Typical Grandma, she said, 'Let's be realistic—I haven't got much longer."

"That *does* sound like her," Pauline laughed. "And the children?" Oh, to be able to ask that question of my own daughter!

"Last month they all got chicken pox, but that's okay. Now it 's out of the way before Matt starts kindergarten. I'm glad of that. I've been thinking about what distinct personalities they have. Matt's the solemn intellectual, Kenny's mellow and placid, Marika's the stubborn live-wire. It makes me wonder how another three would turn out. How long before you start repeating?"

"Tempted to find out?"

"No, thanks. I'll just have to wonder. Are you enjoying the Book of Job? You did skip to that, didn't you?"

Pauline grabbed her Bible and searched for the quote she wanted.

"How about this? With slight changes, of course. 'My breath is [not yet] corrupt, my days are [not] extinct, the graves are [not] ready for me."

"That sounds just like you," Mara laughed.

"Would Hazel agree?"

"Never. She talks like the grave is nearly ready, even though she acts like there are tons of things which need doing."

Pauline felt suddenly somber, and she closed her eyes, picturing a thin, young tree.

"An old friend planted a cottonwood near Jerry's ball park, and part of me thinks that's funny because he'll never live to see it grow up," she said. Mara was quiet. "But part of me thinks that's only right, to live as though you'll last forever. Who knows?"

The two of them were silent, a little surprised, Pauline thought, to find themselves considering such an ancient philosophical question.

Scrapbook, page 18

Glued across the top of this page is a newspaper clipping. The picture is of Mara pushing a double stroller with the twins craning forward, looking around them, and Matt walking next to his mother, fist gripping the metal handle of the stroller. Mara, striding purposefully, is carrying a picket sign, Matt another. Mara's sign is turned so that only the letters ROTC can be seen, but Matt's sign is clearly visible: STOP THE WAR TOYS! Mara's mouth is open, not angrily but calmly, as if she is chanting, joining other voices in the long line ahead of her.

There is no article, only a wide caption that explains that the march occurred last Wednesday in front of the attack helicopter and ROTC recruiting tables and numbered 50 non-violent protesters. Did the reporter count only adults? Matt understood where he was and would have wanted to be counted.

On the left below the article is a yellow telephone message, CITY COLLEGE printed across the top.

M—

Friday—Pauline called. Has sold house! Something about Curly Hair's uncle?? Sounded excited. Call her tonight.—L

Below the telephone message is a postcard, taped only across the top so that the writing on the back can be read.

Darlings, [Pauline's script writes]

Here I am, safe and—sound? The city seems green and everyone's been friendly. Eager to find my way around. More later—

Love and XXOO,
Pauline

Printed in tiny letters up the side of the card are the words: *No fences!!*

The city she is referring to is labeled in gold across the front: KNOXVILLE, and the photo shows brick buildings on wide green lawns—unbroken by any barriers to hospitality—sloping down to a curving river.

Trips to the High Desert have ended. Sitting beneath the cottonwood trees, climbing Goat Mountain, swooping along the roller coaster roads with a comfortable patio waiting ahead—over. Like cutting off the right side of a picture, Mara will limit her vision, not extending it as far east as the desert. With the telephone, she can certainly remain in touch with Tennessee, but Pauline is now within her daughter's orbit.

Centered on the bottom is a final photograph, this one of Mara and Richard holding the twins, none of them smiling. At their feet lies a dog and one cat. A short, plump woman is kissing Matt, who is too big to be in her arms like that but must enjoy grabbing her around the neck, dangling his long, slender legs from her hips. Behind them is a packed car, and across the bottom of the picture is lettered in firm print: HOW CAN ROSIE LEAVE US?

Rosie *and* Pauline, two people important to Mara's functioning. One has enabled her to keep up her daily routine for years, surviving chicken pox and schedules. The other, a sympathetic supporter, has given her another adult to love.

How will she fill the gaps they leave?

Chapter 16

Turning from her dresser, Pauline walked to the bedroom door and looked over her new apartment, trying hard to be happy with what she saw. On the left was what Anne called a "living area"—not a separate room with walls and a door, but just a sofa, a coffee table and a television, the sofa's back creating the line of a narrow walkway into the "dining area." Anne had bought her a vinyl-topped dinette set—strange after owning a heavy maple table which sat eight, but so far this small set had needed to accommodate only her, and it was plenty large enough for that. The narrow kitchen counter was filled by the slow cooker and the coffee maker which Anne had bought to welcome her and on the small space of wall hung the telephone.

Behind me, Pauline thought, is my bedroom, barely big enough for a double bed, a chest and a chair. Gone is Jerry's beloved king size—well, it just would never fit and since the new owner of the house wanted it, why pay to move such a thing? Iona had dismissed it with her hand, unconvinced by Pauline's explanation about why the bed wasn't included in the auction.

"Who'd want that monster?" Iona had bellowed, and Pauline had moved the large SOLD sign into a more prominent spot at the foot of the bed. It had hurt her to think that people might assume no one wanted what she'd loved. Ironically, a SOLD sign had made her feel better. She'd left for a farewell luncheon before most of the buyers arrived— "faster than a painter's elbow" she'd told Anne— and was relieved to find when she returned that the man running the auction had packed into his truck all the items bearing red SOLD stickers so that she wouldn't have to see the marks of…scavengers. I shouldn't think of them that way, she'd chided herself, but there it is.

Next to my tiny bedroom is my tiny bathroom, and that's my whole place, she thought, moving toward the kitchen counter. The best thing about it is the door leading out to the yard. The dark wood has a small pet door cut into the bottom, so Sniffy can go in and out. He's explored this new place more than I have. He's even got a pal already, an adorable little thing who's begun to follow him back in for food. One day I'll learn where that creature belongs, but for now, Sniffy's happy and I don't mind the company…until I have my own friends…however long that takes.

"Mrs. Halperin? This is Betty Taylor from Morningview Hospital. How are *you* today?"

Pauline turned off the burner and sat down at her dinette, telephone against her ear and a half-smile on her face.

"Just fine, thanks," Pauline answered. "You're the woman in charge of volunteers, aren't you?"

"I certainly am," Betty answered cheerfully. "We met last week at the market. Your daughter introduced us. I was hoping to interest you in working at the hospital. Do you think you could give us any time?"

Pauline sat for a moment, stunned by her first telephone call from someone who lives here. A Southerner has reached out to me! Amazing. They must really need volunteers at the hospital.

"Please forgive me, Betty, but I'm still getting used to the idea that you called! I've gone to church three Sundays in a row and no one's said one word to me."

There was a hesitation and then, "I'm so sorry you've encountered rudeness, Pauline." Betty's voice was still polite and Pauline wondered, only briefly, if anyone could say *anything* which would make Betty nasty.

"No, not rude. People just seem private here. More private than back home."

"You're from California, didn't Anne tell me?"

"And now I know what's meant by western hospitality. We try to make people feel welcome, especially if they're strangers." Holy heck, Pauline thought, now I'm all choked up. And why am I talking like this to a woman I hardly know?

"*We* spend our time with our families." Betty's comment, spoken so gently but firmly, reduced the lump in Pauline's throat immediately. "In fact, that's close to why I was calling, to see if you'd work in the waiting room in pediatrics."

Pauline wiped her eyes and took a deep breath.

"I'd love to," she said. "What days do you need me?"

Betty shifted easily to dates and times and ended their conversation by urging Pauline to see the Great Smoky Mountains.

"They're really beautiful," she said, "and there are some wonderful tours. My friends spoke highly of the accommodations. You must explore that."

After hanging up, Pauline sat staring at the telephone. Betty didn't offer to take me or go with me on a tour. It's almost as though she hopes, now that she's made a suggestion, someone else will take care of me.

Down here, Pauline thought, words may be the only thing you get.

"The waiting room is absolutely depressing," Pauline admitted to her daughter over dinner. They sat together, without Fred, in Anne's dining room, furnished with the mahogany table, chairs and sideboard, which had belonged to Pauline's mother. "No color, no pretty paintings, completely bare. They're all set to begin decorating, and it's not a moment too soon, I'd say. But wonderful people, just the finest doctors and nursing staff. I'd take my grandchild there with complete confidence."

Anne leaned back in her chair and smiled.

"If you had a grandchild," she said, and Pauline flushed, face matching her volunteer jacket.

"Well," she said, standing with her plate, "I must get back downstairs. You have work to do."

Anne yawned and arched her back.

"Not so much tonight, fortunately. And it looks like I won't have to fly to Japan after all."

"What a shame!" Pauline cried.

"What a relief!" Anne corrected, walking toward her study. "I can use the time to work on my presentation for the Hudson Company."

Pauline stacked their plates in the sink and turned on the water to rinse them. I don't understand how having a job assignment can spoil one's enjoyment of a foreign country, she thought, and I don't really understand what a presentation is like. Sample ads, that sort of thing, I suppose. Someday, I must get Anne to practice on me so I can get an idea.

She clicked the dishwasher door and headed for the stairs down to her apartment. Not understanding is like being far away, she thought, and it's awful to be far away from one's own daughter, especially when the daughter lives right upstairs.

The couple sat on the small floral couch, staring past their clutched hands at the pale carpet. Although they'd brought in their baby girl only a few hours ago, their clothes were rumpled, as though they hadn't slept in days.

Seeing them looking haggard and distraught, Pauline decided to call the chaplain. He'll know just how to comfort them, she thought. I'm awfully glad this room is painted and furnished now. There's even a private consultation area, where the chaplain can take the parents if they want. Although they're alone, she thought. It's not a big room, but they're the only ones in it, so he can sit right there.

She'd set up a system with the chaplain: beep him and he'd know to come to the waiting room, she'd glance toward the person she wanted him to talk with, he'd walk slowly by several spots, nodding, smiling, saying a few words, and then finally sit down with the designated person. Reverend Munsey and Pauline liked their system because the person never knew the chaplain had been sent for. Perfect.

"Your little girl is Sandy," Rev. Munsey was saying as Pauline came in with a tray of coffee cups and a plate of cookies. Setting down the tray, she backed up a few steps but didn't leave.

The woman nodded and closed her eyes tightly, but her husband leaned forward for a coffee cup and thanked Pauline.

"We brought her in early this morning," he explained. to the chaplain "She fell off our bed and hit the back of her head."

The woman began to cry, hunching into a tight ball, and Pauline moved to hug her, while the husband continued talking.

"The doctor isn't encouraging. They're doing all they can—they have her hooked up to tubes and machines and monitors—I don't know what else they could be doing." He frowned and began to wring his hands. "But she isn't responding. She ought to have opened her eyes by now, but she—she…"

Suddenly bending close to his wife, he began to cry also, quiet, choking sounds like hers.

The chaplain rubbed their hands between his own and waited.

"She has the best possible care," he said when they had quieted, his bushy gray eyebrows arching as his chin dropped and his voice lowered. "And you're nearby, giving her all the love you can. She knows that. Somewhere inside, your love is reaching her."

The woman looked up, her face anxious.

"Do you think the Lord wants my baby?" she cried. "Why would He want her? She's only eight months old! What can it prove?"

Pauline leaned forward also, eager to hear the chaplain's answer, but he only shook his head.

"We can never understand His reasoning."

"That's not for us, Jean," her husband added, grabbing her hand, and the woman began to cry again.

"Would you like me to pray with you?" the chaplain asked, and Pauline was relieved when they nodded. She loved hearing the chaplain's deep voice reciting the 23rd Psalm, especially "...I will fear no evil, for thou art with me." He made her believe, just his person and his manner made her feel a conviction, which carried over to the Bible Study Class. The minister of her church, along with people in the class, would take turns reading aloud—now they were reading the Psalms—but she always imagined how Rev. Munsey would sound. Was that wrong? Would God be angry that she preferred one minister to another?

A nurse called to the couple and they hurried down the hall, staying close to the nurse. Pauline turned to the chaplain.

"The Lord is their light and their salvation," she quoted, hoping that he would be pleased by her knowledge, perhaps talk with her, rub her hands, ease her loneliness. Not a physical sickness, certainly. She almost assured him that she knew she didn't have a life-threatening condition. But it was a loneliness so strong that it was almost a physical pain. She longed for the companionship of old friends, for a younger body, for her husband. That was it, mainly. She longed for Jerry and all that life with him had meant.

And so she would appreciate Rev. Munsey's attention and his voice rolling over her as he spoke the words of the Bible.

Instead, he walked glumly to the door, hands shoved deep into his pockets.

"That child is going to die, Pauline," he said. "Shit."

Mara sounded subdued, and that was fine with Pauline. Before Mara's call, Pauline had dialed the hospital and had confirmed the chaplain's prediction: during the night, Sandy had died. Rev. Munsey was at the parents' home. Except for Sniffy's occasional whining, Pauline cried alone.

"I'm sorry to call with such bad news, Pauline."

"Bad news?" Pauline asked anxiously. "What's happened?"

"Hazel died."

For a moment Pauline couldn't think who Hazel was.

"Grandma Hazel," Mara repeated. "She died in her sleep, I guess. A neighbor found her."

"Oh, my goodness. I'm so sorry, Mara. I know you were very fond of her. How old was she?"

"Eighty-seven."

"So she'd had a long life."

"Yes, very long and very good."

"And she died peacefully? No sign of..." How awful, she thought, stopping herself. I've been working at a hospital too long.

"Quietly. Apparently, she just fell asleep and didn't waken, and I'm glad for that, of course. But Richard's not here. He's taken the kids car camping, so he won't find out until he comes home tomorrow. Meanwhile..."

"Meanwhile, you're wandering around feeling lonely. I know how that goes, believe me."

They were both silent.

"We're connected by more than a telephone, you know, Mara." Pauline hesitated, then asked, "Would you like me to read from the Bible for us?"

To Pauline's amazement, Mara answered, "Yes." So Pauline pulled her worn Bible across the vinyl dinette, opened by chance to Psalm 143, and read as richly as she could.

"…'Therefore is my spirit overwhelmed within me; my heart within me is desolate…"

But after the eighth verse, she stopped. Asking to be delivered from enemies, asking for anyone to be destroyed at a time like this, just didn't seem right.

Scrapbook, page 19

A blank page—this one in memory of Hazel.

Scrapbook, page 20

This page has only three items:

First, a copy of the Memorial Service program. On the cover is a bouquet of lavender flowers above Hazel's name. Inside, one can read that a minister, perhaps from her church, presided, but the unusual thing was a performance of the Brahms Clarinet Quintet by Richard and four other musicians. Hazel may not have understood Brahms, but she would have appreciated the gesture, the serious effort.

Following the music, Mara spoke on "Memories of My Grandmother," but no copy of her remarks is taped here. How much did she choose to include? Could she recognize the threads which came through Hazel's son, inched through Mara and then drifted randomly through Hazel's great grandchildren, carrying preferences, tastes, loves? Perhaps having kept a scrapbook had helped Mara to identify those things, which were most valuable about a valuable person.

Below the small program is a condolence card from Pauline. On the cover in delicate script is printed WITH DEEPEST SYMPATHY and written inside is her note:

Dear Ones, [Pauline writes]

> *My heart goes out to you all. I'm sorry to have read from that Psalm, Mara—it wasn't quite right, which is one more example of my good intentions gone awry—but I haven't been at this Bible study long enough to know what's appropriate, I guess. I took it up because of Jerry and I continue because of me—it's beautiful language and comforting, when a*

person picks the right part to read, which I probably didn't.

    But you know I love you all and am thinking of you. I hope the plant arrived.

Love,
Pauline

On the bottom of the page is glued a heavy note card signed by Loreen. Centered on it are only these words:

Darling, [Loreen writes]
Beautiful. Many thanks.
Love,
Mom

Did Loreen give to her daughter, the grandchild, responsibility for planning Hazel's memorial service? What must this note indicate about Loreen? Did she appreciate Mara's relationship with Hazel? Did she recognize that the young woman knew Loreen's mother-in-law better than she herself did? Did she feel envy, sorrow, regret, or just relief?

What is perhaps more important, what does the note, as well as the program, tell about Mara, her grandmother, their love?

Mara Leeds

Chapter 17

Mara squinted at the numbers on the buildings, her search hampered by the unfamiliar neighborhood. Where is this place? she thought. I only come out here to go to the Burbank Airport, never to shop. I should have invited Christy—she knows the Valley.

By closing first one eye and then the other, Mara could confirm that her right eye wasn't blurry anymore. Just buy a cane, she told herself, and go on climbing the stairs to graduate classes for the next couple years until I have my administrative credential, and then re-evaluate. See how I am, what I want to do. Cheerful and up-beat, that's my attitude. After all, this may not get any worse.

Suddenly, there it was, the name spelled out in large letters above the door: CANE HOUSE. Mara parked, noticing the height of the curb. That's something I never cared about before, she thought, but now I hope for smooth pathways. Tossing her purse over her shoulder, she took the large step while steadying herself with one hand on the trunk of her car, then looked back to see her handprint in the dust. May I live in a land of smooth inclines or cheap carwashes, she thought, and pushed open the shop's glass door.

The clerk was brisk and well-informed, glancing at the check mark in the catalogue in Mara's hand before carefully lifting a cane from the rack on the wall.

"Good choice," she said. "This is your most classic. Unobtrusive."

Mara held the shiny wood stick with gold trim and extended it in front of her.

"Unobtrusive?" she questioned. "How can someone using a cane not attract attention?"

The clerk didn't answer but instead twisted the cane in Mara's grip and measured with her eyes.

"It's not the right height, of course," she said. "I'd have to use the tape and then the cane is specially made for you. But as canes go, it's the most classic style. Or there's this one," she said, grabbing a cane covered with tiny blue flowers inside a polyurethan coating. "You could begin with one color and ask for the others later. For Christmas, say."

Mara felt peculiar. Didn't this woman care about why she needed one at all? Whether she'd even have time to accumulate all the colors? Wouldn't need make a difference in the choice?

Before the clerk could hand her a third cane, Mara announced, "I have multiple sclerosis. M.S."

The woman grabbed a solid black cane with a gold duck's head.

"I've got some leg weakness," Mara continued, forcing herself to talk calmly, "so I thought a cane might help me cover longer distances."

The woman nodded and fitted the duck's head into Mara's hand.

"No," she said, pulling it away, "too masculine. I really think the oak one is your best bet, or one of the fabrics."

Mara tried again.

"I'll probably use a cane a lot if the M.S. gets worse."

Without responding, the woman held up two canes, one with the floral pattern against a blue background, the other against green.

"Of course, these might conflict with your outfit," she said.

Mara gave up. This woman isn't going to react. I could want the cane for vanity as easily as need, and it's all the same to this shop. I'm a sale, that's all.

The woman tried out several lengths before recording Mara's number, encouraged her to order a wrist strap, and then walked briskly to the cash register.

"Your cane length is on file here," she assured Mara as she punched buttons, "so if you ever want a collapsible cane for traveling or one of those fabric styles, just call. Meanwhile, you'll receive a card in a week or so to come pick up your cane, all properly sized for you."

Feeling devilish, Mara opened to the catalogue's first page.

"Could I just see one of those?" she asked and pointed to the cane described as "made from a breeding bull's stretched penis."

The clerk glanced at the picture, then looked away.

"We don't carry those," the clerk said coldly, extending Mara's receipt. "Thank you."

Pity, Mara thought, as she carefully stepped off the curb, leaving yet another print on her car's trunk. The catalogue said they come in varying lengths and widths. Naturally.

The children were asleep and Richard was working late, so Mara could call her friend Christy, describing her request at the cane store.

Christy laughed.

"I wonder if everyone asks to see that one."

"Or no one asks," Mara said. "Anyway, at least I did it."

Christy started several sentences.

"No, no," Mara explained, "I mean buying a cane. It's a symbol."

"Of what?"

"Acceptance. Reality."

"Vulnerability?" Christy suggested.

Mara was silent. Vulnerability. That was a biggie. Career woman, mother of three, happy occasional homemaker—it's all threatened. From now on, I may need help, various kinds, a changing list of needs.

"It might not ever get too severe," Christy suggested, as though knowing Mara's thoughts. "Isn't that what the doctor said?"

"Attack-remission," Mara confirmed, "but I have the other kind, too. I have attacks, but I also have the chronic-progressive type."

"Which is?"

"Where you slowly but steadily fall apart," Mara answered.

Mara felt guilty saying that. After all, maybe Richard's right, and it would be better not to talk about it. Live up to normality, create a self-fulfilling prophecy. If I start using the word M.S. frequently, or get too comfortable discussing symptoms, it may get worse faster. Pretending to feel fine may force me to feel fine.

"Well," Christy said, her practical voice reassuring to Mara, "let's agree never to discuss this after dark. You can think and read about it all you want during daylight hours, but when the sun goes down, not a word."

Mara laughed in surprise.

"Truly," Christy insisted. "It's one of those topics best considered only in sunshine. I have a whole list of daylight topics."

"Such as?"

"Such as I was supposed to be a boy. My father really wanted a son and he even had the name picked out—Christopher—and then I came along. Surprise, surprise. I don't think he ever forgave me. But if you let me talk about that now, I'll get maudlin and no good will come of it, so let's stop. Do you promise not to think about M.S. after dark?"

Mara hesitated.

"If you're tempted," Christy added, "call me and we can discuss—nasturtiums or my tomato crop or the mayor's wife's hair. Anything! Promise?" she repeated.

"Okay," Mara agreed. Actually, she thought, it sounds like an idea worth trying.

Sitting on Matt's bed, Mara carefully folded his clean clothes. He was just about at the age now where he could choose his own outfits in the morning, she thought—in fact, he'd already insisted a few times—and that would be strange, nice but strange. Meanwhile, still in charge, she patted shirts into one drawer, pants into another, matched the trim around the socks, folded his underpants.

I feel low today, Mara thought. An unexpected limitation, like wobbling in those heels yesterday and buying a pair of flats, makes me feel scared for a while, more than a little sorry for myself. What a roller coaster I'm on now: stiff upper lip one day, like when I bought my cane, then down in the dumps the next.

She could hear the twins playing in their room. Typical, she thought: Kiki demanding all the toys, Ken happy with whatever's left. They won't need a referee for a while, the toys newly discovered since they were put away a few days ago.

"Where's Matt?" Richard asked, appearing in the doorway. "He wanted me to give him another clarinet lesson."

Mara pushed aside some clothes so that Richard could sit beside her.

"I don't know who's luckier, you or Matt. His first lesson was such a wonderful experience for both of you," she laughed.

Richard ran his hand through his hair, and Mara dropped a shirt to touch his hand, then follow the shiny auburn hair to his shoulders. He leaned forward to kiss her.

"I was thinking," he said, rubbing her cheek, "that you should see another doctor, the one that woman suggested. He might have more up-to-date information."

"Richard…"

"Really!   A GP can't know everything, or those specialists.   Bladders, eyes, ears—that's all they know! How can they be sure about something neurological?"

"Richard—"

"Even if you have to pay, I mean if our insurance won't cover it, I think you should go."

Mara swallowed and squeezed his hand. I know what he's doing, she thought. I know enough about the grieving process to recognize denial.

"I will," she said, "but I'm afraid Dr. McIntyre's right. Don't get your hopes up, that I can take a pill and be all better."

"But you don't know," Richard protested.

He's frightened, Mara thought. Underneath the up-beat exterior, so am I.

"I was thinking about the remodeling," she said. "Maybe we shouldn't do it." There. Fear expressed.

Richard looked at her quickly, alarmed.

"I mean,: she continued, "we don't know how much longer I'll be able to work—"

"Mara!"

"It's true," she insisted. "I just don't feel good about taking on a new debt."

This is being cautious, she thought. As Dr. McIntyre had advised, being prudent.

Richard turned to face her.

"You're not going to have to stop working any time soon, maybe ever."

Some things we say for ourselves as much as for the other person, Mara thought. Looking into his eyes, she willed his conviction to be absorbed through her skin so that she could feel more confident. She wanted to believe with him that she could go on, the routines would be ever so slightly affected, the cane would stay locked in the trunk, unneeded. After all, he'd said to her when she'd tried to display it, you have *me*.

"So we go ahead with the room," he added. "Life doesn't stop because you have some—problem."

"But we have to use our heads," Mara insisted, suddenly close to tears. It seems superficial, she thought, but after the high heels go, what follows?

Richard stood, looking stern and—resolute, Mara thought.

"Life doesn't stop," he repeated and left her surrounded by Matt's clothes.

"Being old is the pits, Mara," Pauline said the next day. She liked calling on Sundays: it was cheaper, of course, but it was more than that. Sunday was a talking day to her. It should be devoted to conversations, especially with old friends.

"I think the worst part about it is the not knowing," she continued. "You can't count on the body anymore or on the brain remembering anything. You don't know what tomorrow holds."

"Young people think they control the future. It's all a result of their own effort." These conversations have special meaning to me now, Mara thought, but Pauline doesn't know that yet.

"You're right," Pauline said. "At the first look-see, it's not so bad, being in your seventies, if you have a loving family and friends who care about you. Who ever asked an old lady to go out in the rain for some milk? But then, you have pains and you lock yourself out of the house and your daughter doesn't want you driving anymore. I hate being so dependent!" she continued. "Anne wonders why I struggle over to the hospital to volunteer, but no one wants to feel useless, Mara! If I didn't do that much, I'd be a miserable blob."

Mara understood. Pauline couldn't know how well she understood.

"Don't you think connections are helping?" Mara asked.

"Definitely."

"I saw that with Grandma, how her causes kept her mind working."

"They do. Even if it's just a little unpaid job, that's a lifeline. And driving—vital for the morale."

Mara pictured her own car.

"Does a cane help? Or a walker?" she asked.

Pauline was exasperated. She hated remembering herself with the walker.

"Pooh! I don't *want* to be old, Mara. That's all there is to it!"

"I can appreciate that, but you'll need to accept the assistance of people or objects so that you can continue. You want to function—"

"Definitely!" Pauline said again.

"So let yourself be old. Let yourself need help. You've earned it."

"Let myself be old," Pauline repeated. "Now there's a pearl! How can such a statement make me feel better? I mean, it's sort of—sad."

Mara laughed.

"I'm glad I said something useful, even if it *is* sad!"

Pauline thought of what she'd been reading.

"Even in laughter, the heart is sorrowful," she quoted.

"Surprise! I have a Bible right here. Where is that?"

"You do? Well, isn't that something. Proverbs 14, verse…let me find it, verse 13."

Mara found the spot and finished the quote: "…and the end of that mirth is heaviness."

"Sorry," Pauline laughed. "I seem to have a knack for quoting grim words from the Bible."

Sitting by the phone a moment later, Mara re-read the words: 'Even in laughter, the heart is sorrowful, and the end of that mirth is heaviness.' The words fit. My joking is a cover, almost an escape.

While she'd been talking, the sun had set and the windows had become dark. She thought of Christy's daylight topics. Well, she thought, I knew, especially at first, that it would be a difficult promise to keep.

Scrapbook, page 21

This page is devoted to children. In the top right corner is a copy of IQ test results for Mathew Albert Leeds, QUALIFIED stamped in red letters across the scores. Leading down to a typed list labeled GIFTED PROGRAM—GRADE 1 is a piece of yellow yarn. The list includes field trips, art instruction, even a band. An irregular circle in thick brown crayon has been drawn around that word—Matt must have decided what he likes.

Yellow yarn continues to a photo of the twins swinging in a playground filled with large rubber ducks, a row of wooden teeter totters, and a giant box of plastic bats and hula hoops. With their dad pushing them on the swings, the children are grinning, happy for his attention, happy to be living in a world filled with nothing but toys.

Green yarn stretches down to five red and blue circus ticket stubs. Another pair—for children? adults to help supervise?—is off to the side, as though Mara needs only that inch of space setting off the two tickets to remind her of the event, who went, who ate what, who needed to rush for the potty, who was frightened by the roar of the lions.

Yellow and green yarn twists up to a photograph taken with props from the wild west. Richard and Mara's faces, mock and somber, stick through circular holes above cardboard outits, hers a flouncy dress with low bodice trimmed in lace, his the black hat, shirt, pants, and silver buckle to set off a gleaming gun in its holster. Next to them are three smaller faces with crazy grins and shiny, dark eyes above cardboard outfits depicting a barroom dancer, a cowboy and a child dressed for church. Their faces, as always, look delighted to be where they are, doing what they are doing.

Yellow yarn ends in a drawing done by one or all of the children, a drawing which includes no people, only a fence and a table with four rickety chairs, and animals, everywhere fluffy cats and dogs rolling, playing with each other, with balls, with sticks, with fabric mice. Glued onto one mouse's whiskers are pieces of green thread.

The whole page is a riot of color and texture, a statement about families and fun, a tribute to the brightness, which children have added to one couple's life.

Chapter 18

The trick, Mara thought as she pulled into Staff Parking, is not to get—as Christy would say—maudlin. Work at the Women's Clinic should help. And painting again. Standing in front of an easel, holding out the brush to measure—wait. Can I still stand like that?

Mara sat motionless behind the wheel. She hadn't pictured the physical act of painting, only remembered that it had always brought her intense pleasure, partly because she knew and everyone told her that she was good, and also because it would give her something to do while Richard taught the children how to hike or ski or whatever else he had in mind. Well, she thought, dropping the keys in her purse, a stool should be enough.

The walk to the cafeteria was long, and she almost tripped, one foot dragging a little. Grabbing a light pole, she stared up at the old-fashioned fixture, pretending to be fascinated by its design before loosening her grip and walking on, hoping she appeared—not drunk, but in love with lamps. Once in the cafeteria, she waved at her colleague, Bea Paredo, who'd already located a table for them.

"What a hell of a week," Bea said, throwing her sweater and books on the floor before rubbing her eyes. "Every day we've had pickets at the Clinic, carrying all their pathetic signs about babies. I wonder how many of them would adopt two or three."

Mara shook her head.

"I've thought the same. Another thing is, I don't like to see men on an abortion picket line. It's almost—I don't know—"

"None of their damn business," Bea finished, emphasizing her words by breaking a donut into chunks.

Mara sipped her coffee. Bea could slim down, she thought, if she'd stop eating those donuts, but somehow the weight suits her. Her big brown eyes with their long lashes could make it easy for someone to trivialize her, assume that she's superficial. The girth sets you straight, as well as her low, blunt voice.

"So you're starting work at the Clinic this weekend?" Bea asked.

"Yeah. Both mornings. Anything I should know?"

"Just be prepared. I'm sure the lines will be there."

"I have a pregnant student I'm trying to talk into some counseling. She may run away the minute she sees a picket sign."

"Who's the girl?"

Mara wondered briefly if her conversation with Rachel had been confidential. Probably, but this is a woman who can help, and it's a shame not to seek her advice.

"Rachel Reid. You know the one who wrote that poem about loss for the literary magazine?"

"I liked that poem." Bea shook her head. "Why is it always the sensitive types who get into trouble? 'I didn't want to reject him,' they say later. Well, foolish or not, they deserve our help."

"I don't think the daddy is even a boyfriend, just a date. Now what?"

Bea began chewing a second donut.

"Now she learns from her mistake. She gets an abortion and never looks back. She finishes her AA, transfers to a university, maybe moves so the jerk can't find her. The key is, she doesn't let this mess up her life. She had plans and she should stick to them."

"That was fast!"

Bea stirred her coffee.

"I know because I've been there. You are looking at the product of a mixed marriage who herself had a mixed baby out of wedlock. Only my son died, and with him part of me died, too."

Mara sat stunned, but Bea, apparently oblivious, continued.

"I waffled around and cursed the daddy who didn't care and had screaming hassles with my folks because they acted relieved and flunked out of school and spent two years finding myself. But—" she said, leaning forward "—when I did, I never looked back."

Mara watched Bea put the last of the donut into her mouth. Jung said that everyone has some experience which he spends the rest of his life trying to figure out, Mara thought. Maybe that was hers.

"How old were you?" Mara asked.

"Seventeen. Terrific age for childbearing, the books say. Well, you can tell Rachel that being 17 makes pregnancy easy on the body, but nothing else is ready. Trust me. Nothing! So she'll be coming in?"

Mara nodded.

"She hopes someone can help her decide if she should tell the guy, maybe marry him, whether to tell her parents and move back home, if they'll let her, whether to quit school—"

"Ha!" Bea exploded. "Not expecting much, is she? You don't mention the main concern: whether to have the baby at all."

"That too," Mara said quietly.

"No, no, my friend, that's *her* decision. Don't let anyone else take responsibility for that one."

Mara sighed. What if Rachel didn't come or was scared away by the picketers?

As though reading her mind, Bea said, "She shouldn't try to go it alone. That doesn't work, not with important stuff. I don't mean you stand up on top of the bell tower and announce your crisis to the world, but you tell someone, and then you let that person help, which may mean bringing in some other people. Believe me, when I wanted to get my life back together, it took a ton of people pushing and pulling. I'm not one of those 'Stay away, I can do it myself!' people. We're human beings, so we need each other. We work in a group. You know what I mean?"

The cafeteria was almost empty. Bea spoke forcefully, sounding, Mara felt, like a person made wise by experience, not only hers, but everyone's.

"Speaking of secrets," Mara said, "I want to tell you something."

Bea slapped a palm to her forehead.

"Dear Lord in heaven, you're not pregnant again, are you?"

"Nothing like that. I—well—"

Bea raised one hand, flecked with crumbs.

"Hold it! I have a class right now, and if you unload, I won't be able to be my usual, brilliant self."

Throwing her paper cup and saucer into the trash, she shrugged into her sweater.

"Meet me in an hour, same place. No, wait, I have an appointment with Danny. Could we get together at six?"

Mara gathered her books and walked with Bea toward the swinging doors.

"I have to pick up the kids. Really—"she insisted, when Bea began to apologize—"we'll talk some other day. Will you be working at the clinic on Saturday?"

Bea squeezed her arm. "I plan to be there," she said.

Rachel came around the corner just as Mara was walking to the entrance. Seeing her, Mara tripped in a sidewalk crack, put her arm around Rachel's shoulders and hurried her past the few picketers into the clinic.

"Thank God there aren't many today. They must sleep late on Saturdays."

Pale, Rachel looked around the waiting room. What is she expecting? Mara wondered. She was dressed in jeans and a baggy sweatshirt, and Mara thought again how the styles allow pregnant women to hide longer than in the past. Looking at her, I'd never guess, except that she looks so frightened.

"The picketers won't come inside," Mara said reassuringly, but Rachel didn't answer. Mara noticed that the cloth band around her ponytail was hanging loose, as though she had been in a hurry this morning.

Leaning over the desk, Mara began to grab forms, trying to remember what she'd been taught.

"You need to fill these out," she said. "In ink. Sorry there are so many, but—"

Abruptly, Rachel turned toward the door.

"Never mind, Mrs. Leeds. I think this was a mistake."

"Don't leave!" Mara cried and grabbed her arm. "Forget the forms! Let me take you straight to a counselor and you can get started. We'll do the paperwork later."

With Mara pushing, Rachel resisting slightly, they moved down the narrow hall to the first open door.

"Rachel," Mara said, "this is Bea."

Standing, Bea extended her hand, then waved toward the chair.

"Congratulations," she said and grinned broadly at Rachel. "We were worried that you might not make it."

Rachel looked from Bea to Mara, smiling slightly.

"You'll enjoy talking with her," Mara said. "She's really experienced with—well—" Mara shrugged and closed the door behind them.

Walking back to the front desk, Mara decided that Bea had been right. We *are* a group animal, and we shouldn't be afraid of turning to one another. That's in a woman's nature, after all. Striving for connections, she could work for harmony. Everyone would benefit.

Anyway, she thought, the strong women in my life have valued their impact. I will, too.

Sitting at the scuffed brown reception desk, Mara began to fill in what she could on Rachel's forms.

Scrapbook, page 22

Lettered across the top of this page, to help Mara remember but probably not to help the page make sense to others, are the words SEEMINGLY UNRELATED—BUT RELATED.

The first item is an appointment slip for the Women's Clinic. "Dr. Magnis" is checked, a date is written in, and next to "Patient's Name" is RACHEL RIE—then a diagonal line. The last name must have been misspelled, the paper torn from its pad and crumpled, perhaps tossed in the basket only to be retrieved and shoved into Mara's pocket or purse.

Directly below is a card from a floral arrangement. Written in bold script are simply the words WE'LL TACKLE THIS TOGETHER—LOVE, BEA. The bouquet honors—what? Mara must have made time to confide, confess fears. Perhaps Bea had been horrified, then strong and assured, helping her to resolve uncertainties. The bouquet acknowledges the support offered by friends.

Next is a slip of paper. APPLICATION FOR SPECIAL PARKING it reads, and Mara has filled in the blanks, including REASON, where she has printed MS. The red APPROVED stamp must indicate that she may now park on the "Study Skills Center Driveway."

Last is a second florist card, this one saying, YOU'RE SPECIAL TO US ALL. HAPPY BIRTHDAY—RICHARD

How are these items related? One answer might be "acceptance," each item indicating that some terms with reality have been made. Another answer might be "connections," each indicating a reaching out, a recognition of a link. A third might be simply "Big Events," each symbolizing something significant for Mara.

Perhaps none is right—that is, what Mara had in mind. But then, who is to say that only she is accurate in interpreting her own life?

Chapter 19

This view is breathtaking, Mara thought, stopping by the stream. Not that it's overwhelming, like some of Ansel Adams' photographs or the lavish staging of one of Mrs. D.'s operas, but it's lush and peaceful. The stream meanders through the meadow, thick with grasses made green by regular rain. One or two fishermen approach its banks each day, hollering when they pull in a dark, flapping trout. Around the edge of the meadow is a ring of sheer mountains, dotted with ski lifts unmoving in the summer. The sky is soft and clear, and the few cars traveling the closest highway barely disturb the quiet. This is where I want to be, always.

It's painful knowing that, Mara thought as she stood quietly. As long as I'm working, I'm too busy to pass judgment on my surroundings, whether L.A. is really where I want to live, or tutoring college students is really how I want to work, or whether the congested market is where I want to buy the week's groceries. But once I slow down for a vacation, look out! Suddenly, alternatives pop up, and I see other people go about their lives making other choices, and then I ask myself: Am I really forced to live as I do, or is it basically a choice I've made?

Seeing this spot, this semi-wilderness, Mara knew the ideal and how far from this beauty she ordinarily lived. It was difficult accepting that.

For several summers, she and Richard had vacationed here, renting a house from a woman they'd never met, although they'd decided, judging from her telephone voice, her underwear left in a drawer and the magazines stacked below the sink, that she could probably fit the word bawdy. It was an overstuffed, well-used house, filled with found-art, comfortable and child-proof, and their only annoyance was in answering the twins' incessant questions about the peculiar objects nailed high on the walls or hanging from thick wires over the large wood slab which was a dining table. For a week or two, they relaxed, unconcerned about scratches, bangs or an answering machine.

"Paradise," Richard had shaken his head as he pulled on heavy socks for a hike. "It may be a pain getting away, but I'm always glad to be here."

The four of them tramped off down the meadow, holding hands as they headed for the red cliffs, and left Mara to paint. The twins won't go as far as they've bragged that they can, Mara thought as she unfolded her easel and positioned the three wobbly legs on a firm place in the meadow. But they'd rather stick with Daddy—there's more chance of having a fascinating adventure with him than with me.

So. Already, in my young children's eyes, I'm predictably no fun. So be it, she thought, snapping open her wooden paint case and preparing her pallet. I just have to pursue my loves and hope they appreciate me for it later, when they're interested in more than adventure. Pulling over the stool which Matt had carried, she felt it sink into the dirt as she carefully balanced herself.

"And you know what else?" Kiki cried. "We saw where there was a fire!"

Matt turned toward Mara, nodding in serious confirmation of his sister's words.

"Dad said it was—how long ago, Dad? When was the fire?"

Richard finished chewing, then swallowed a gulp from his wine glass. The large dining plank was cluttered with napkins, paper towels, plates of chicken and salad, milk in glasses and some in rings marking the wood, scattered serving spoons and a half-empty bottle of wine. Surveying her family and the mess, Mara felt glad to be past the high chair stage. Cleaning up the table was bad enough without having to vacuum the carpet.

"1974," Richard answered. "Destroyed thousands of acres around here. But you have to understand," he added for Matt's benefit, since the twins were already climbing down from their chairs and leaving the table, "Nature needs occasional fires to thin out the forests and all the undergrowth."

"You're not referring to manmade fires," Mara interjected.

"No, no, just the natural ones. They're usually caused by lightening."

Matt looked from one to the other, his hazel eyes thoughtful.

"So sometimes bad things do good," Matt concluded.

Richard nodded and went on to describe the good which came from forest fires, but Mara sat thinking. Emerson had a theory of compensation. Out of every evil there can come a good, a benefit from every tragedy, he had written. According to his philosophy, it was only fitting that Mara's father's death had given her welcome distance from her mother, or that the large class had forced her to use small groups more effectively. Suddenly, as Matt and Richard stood to clear the table, she saw the fisherman in the meadow that afternoon, setting down his pole and tackle box to stand behind her and point out exactly what he admired in her painting. To her amazement, he'd asked how much she'd want for it.

"Once it's done to your liking, of course," he had said. "I trust that you and I have the same taste."

She must have looked blank or flustered because he had dropped a business card on her easel, picked up his gear and sauntered off through the grass.

"I'm staying at the lodge," he'd called over his shoulder. "Just give me a call."

Rinsing the dishes before setting them in rows in the automatic washer, creating a pattern different from the one she'd invented after breakfast, Mara realized that Emerson would say rediscovering her love of painting was compensation for not being able to hike anymore. I could never have earned any money from walking, she thought, or made some man consider his artistic taste. Somehow, I must be benefiting from having a chronic disease.

The idea was troubling, and Mara hurried to escape the solitude of the kitchen, joining her family's nightly card game. Wait until daytime, she advised herself. Consider it then.

"When we built the addition back home, maybe we should have made room for a window seat," Richard said, standing with hands on his hips in the center of the comfortable living room and looking at Mara, stretched out on the window seat. "When you're not standing at an easel—"

"—sitting—"

"—you're reading."

"Those are my outdoor and indoor hobbies, one for each place. Sometimes I add Grandpa's favorite."

"Which was? I forget."

Mara lowered the book to her chest and closed her eyes.

"Napping. I must have inherited the knack."

Richard threw himself down on a nearby sofa and the two of them lay quietly, not responding to the shouts of their children in the loft. The three children were playing a raucous game of ping-pong, the twins against Matt.

"Wow! Did you see that shot?" Matt cried. "You never had a chance. Somebody go get the ball."

"Matt's exerting the privilege of age," Mara whispered, but Richard didn't respond and the two of them remained still as Ken tiptoed by, grabbing the ball off the coffee table.

"Okay. That's 47 to 29," Matt said as the ball began to bounce again.

"They must be inventing new rules," Mara said quietly. Richard opened one eye, then closed it again.

"So what else is new?" he asked.

They lay quietly for several more minutes.

"You going to apply for that job?" Richard suddenly asked.

Mara looked over at him, but he was still stretched out, eyes closed, hands pillowing his head.

"The director job?" She asked, turning onto her side, alert now. "I've been thinking about it a lot."

Richard rolled over to face her, coffee table and chairs separating them.

"And?" he asked.

"It would make getting my administrative credential worthwhile," Mara laughed. Not much of a reason, she thought, but the credential was hard work.

"And I could do the job. I have a zillion ideas." Mara thought of her many sessions with Bea, re-thinking the work of the Center, involving its staff in Freshman Orientation, sponsoring a series of guest lecturers—all of them inspiring role models—even doing more career counseling. All good, do-able ideas, and all which only the director could make happen.

"So why not?" Richard asked.

Mara wondered why not. The room addition had happened. I went to school, taking evening and summer classes, some of which were pretty interesting, until I earned the certificate. I've begun using my cane at work, like a gay coming out of the closet, Bea teased me, and no one has stopped seeking my assistance or advice. I've joined the MS Society and I could, if anyone wanted to hear, which anyone doesn't, spout figures and explanations and summaries. Matt, whom I've told, is growing into a solid, interesting little person, not obviously harmed by knowing that his mother's future is—iffy. Life is going on, and I'm helping that to happen. So why not?

Because, Mara thought, I'm having more physical problems—more unsteadiness, blotchy vision, numbness in my hands and feet—and because I have a neurologist now…I guess I just get frightened—about my future, our future.

Richard was watching her, waiting.

"I think," Mara began in a voice so small that she surprised herself, "I wonder how anyone can prefer me over other candidates."

Richard rolled onto his back and waved one hand.

"But that's natural!" he cried. "Anyone feels a little insecure, unless he's an egomaniac—or a musician, which is probably the same thing."

"No, I mean, wouldn't they want someone…able-bodied? Could I handle the job, physically handle it? Remember, I'd have to work summers. Can I do that? With all the heat?"

Richard was silent.

"I think you should apply," he said finally. "And you know what else?" he asked, sitting up and turning to face her. "I think we should look at the lots for sale around here. That's right—"and he grabbed Ken who was just reaching for the ping-pong ball which had barely missed Richard's head as it sailed onto the couch—"I think we'd be crazy not to at least look into building up here."

Over Ken's bottom, tipped into the air so that his bare feet stuck out, pedaling while he squealed, Richard announced, "You're going to get that job, Mara, and we're both going to take a month off in the summer, and we're coming up here."

He set Ken on his feet, and his son stared at him, wide-eyed.

"To our own house!" Richard said, even more loudly.

"And our own ping pong table?" Ken asked.

Kiki leaned over the railing. "I want my own room!"

"So do I!" Ken cried.

Richard grinned at Mara, and she noticed the crinkles around his eyes and the flecks of gray over his ears. She was pleased to feel such affection for him, even though, she smiled to herself, *I don't know how he voted in the last election.*

"But—" she began, not wanting to spoil the excitement but struggling to stay rooted, "is this really the place for…for…"

Richard leaned toward her.

"If you're going to be stuck in a wheelchair someday, wouldn't you rather be able to look at—"here he waved toward the meadow and the red cliffs—"that?"

Mara smiled. *He makes a wheelchair sound so ordinary,* she thought, and she was relieved.

Suddenly, Matt called down to his parents. "What about forest fires? What if our house catches fire?"

Squeezing Ken, Richard looked up at the loft where his older son hung far over the railing.

"Not likely!" he answered.

"But what if it does?" Matt persisted.

"Well," Richard shrugged, squeezing Ken even more tightly, "then at least we would have enjoyed it while it lasted. Right, Mommy?"

All eyes turned to look at Mara.

"As long as we can, right?" Richard prompted more softly.

Mara realized that he knew the significance of his question, that he knew, although the children couldn't, that he and Mara were finishing an earlier conversation. She looked out the window and heard herself sigh—with a mixture, she thought, of both optimism and sadness.

"Daddy's right," Mara answered. "You enjoy it as long as it lasts."

Delighted, the children screamed, jumping up and down. Some decision had been made, it seemed, some decision which meant separate rooms and their own ping-pong table, and this was worth getting excited about.

Scrapbook, page 23

This page is full of items. First is a business card from Holtzman's Van Conversions, with WIDEN BRAKE PAD—LEEDS—$89 scrawled in ink in the corner. This must be an estimate for a job, perhaps on Mara's car, to make it easier for her to drive using her left foot to reach the pedal without error, so that she could safely brake for pedestrians or children darting into the crosswalk or cats. In that case, Holtzman had provided her a service far more valuable than $89 would indicate.

Below the business card is a small slip of paper, this one a return address carefully cut from an envelope. RACHEL REID, the name says, followed by an address in Long Beach. Rachel and Mara must have become more than student-teacher in order for Mara to have mounted her address. Does she live with parents? With an infant? With—unlikely as it once seemed—with a husband?

Below is a shiny red prize ribbon with FIRST PLACE—LANDSCAPES—MULHOLLAND ART FESTIVAL lettered in silver around the gold foil seal. One of Mara's paintings must have been honored. Almost more than the acclaim is the significance of Mara's decision to enter at all, for successful competition requires preparation and focus, both of which increase self-confidence. Did that ribbon, and what went into winning it, change her?

Continuing in a circle, there is a copy of a FAX which reads with the brisk authority of a telegram:

TO: Mara and Richard Leeds—Owners
This is to confirm that escrow has closed on Lot 125, Pinecrest. Larry Wickes, contractor in the area, will be calling you.

Congratulations.
Nancy Fogerty, Realtor

So they had decided to gamble on buying a piece of their paradise. And did Larry ever reach them, to doodle, to pump them for preferences, such as an open area for a ping pong table, or a cosy window seat?

Squeezed onto the page, slightly overlapping the FAX, is a page torn out of a newsletter from the MS Society, Los Angeles Chapter. Circled in red is the information:

Support Group for Newly Diagnosed
Location: Birnkrant Recreation Center, Hollywood
7 - 9 p.m., Four consecutive Mondays beginning April 2
Leader: Mara Leeds, Director, City College Skills Center

In case one read too quickly, missing the change in title, wedged above this clipping is a taped Polaroid photo of a brightly-lettered banner hanging above a crowd of grinning people, including Richard and Mara's children, all raising glasses to Mara, who sits apart. The banner reads WE COULDN'T BE HAPPIER ABOUT OUR NEW BOSS! and the jubilant people below look like they mean it.

Then Mara applied and was successful. But like the ribbon on the painting, the new title symbolizes more than a victory. It indicates that she has made a decision about limitations and direction, so that her life can now encompass the demands of administration as well as art. This is interesting. This is a big step.

Chapter 20

"I can't talk long, Pauline. I've got to get ready for this little luncheon I'm hosting."

"Who's coming?" Pauline asked, and Mara was amused. Considering that Pauline lives thousands of miles away, she thought, there's a good chance she doesn't know the people. But she does have a wonderful memory for names and details, and she wants to be involved.

"Bea, my friend from work, and Christy, my friend from—well, actually, I met her through Richard. She's Joe's girlfriend. He's another studio musician. I think Bea and Christy'll hit it off really well. They're both a little outrageous. Of course, I guess they could hate each other for the same reason."

Laughing, Mara moved the receiver to cup it with her other shoulder so that she could tear open the bag of crackers for Ken, who was holding it silently up to her. Snack available, he went back outside. Mara glanced at the clock. Just another few minutes and then I *must* hang up, she thought.

"I can't imagine you introducing people who won't have a great time," Pauline said reassuringly. "No men?"

"Not even my sons," Mara answered.

"What are you serving?"

"We've been hearing all the jokes about quiche but we've never eaten it, so I'm serving spinach and mushroom quiche, sausage, muffins and fresh fruit," Mara said.

It's funny, Mara thought, but I know that I could describe a salad made of garden weeds sprinkled with flies and Pauline would assure me that it sounded interesting.

It's funny, Pauline thought, but I know that she could be cooking from a mix and it would be done in some classy way.

"And how are you feeling?" Pauline asked.

Mara hesitated. With Pauline she was always truthful, which took more thought than simply saying, "Oh, fine," as she did with most other people.

"Well, it's hot, so I'm feeling pretty limp," Mara said. "I discovered at Thanksgiving that I can't stand up cooking very long, and that was sobering."

"I know what you mean," Pauline said, remembering the recent holiday and how useless she'd been in Anne's kitchen. "Sometimes I think I do more good just finding a safe, out-of-the-way place to park myself. When I try to help, I'm too shaky and slow, and it just makes Anne cross. Like the other day in the supermarket. I hate taking so long to write a check and then hunting through my wallet for the right card. '*Mo*ther,' she's saying and everyone in the line probably hates me. I know the clerks dread it when I come in."

Mara laughed.

"Does the sign say, 'No one over 70'?"

"I don't believe it does, no."

"Then you take all the time you need. Let them wait. That's the way I feel. Hey, do they want to switch places with you or me? Carry our infirmities? I doubt it. Until then, don't be affected by their impatience. You deserve *some* perk, after all!"

Bravado, Mara thought. That's all I have. But Pauline felt warmed by Mara's assurances.

"Now I must go," Mara said. "I've got to put the quiches in the oven."

"You've already made them?"

"I've already bought them!" Mara laughed wryly. "I told you I can't stand up that long."

"Thank goodness for supermarkets," Pauline said.

"And bakeries."

"And those discount places."

"Like warehouses?" Mara asked.

"Where you can buy enough toilet paper for an army battalion," Pauline said.

"Or enough quiche for three hungry ladies," Mara added.

Opening the oven door a moment later, she realized that she was warmed inside, not by the oven, but by Pauline's acceptance. We both need to hear courage, she thought, and slammed the oven shut.

"Delicious," Bea said, patting her stomach as she stretched out on the couch. "Real men don't know what they're missing."

"I don't know how you did it. All that good food plus Mimosa cocktails," Christy said, kicking off her shoes and sprawling in an oversized rocker. "Correction: I don't want to know. I just want to enjoy." For a moment she closed her eyes, with her bare feet pushing the rocker in time to the Mozart clarinet concerto coming from the radio.

"It's not working," Christy said, opening her eyes and sitting upright.

"What's she blabbing about, Mara?" Bea asked, still slumped into the cushions.

Mara picked up her tall champagne glass and sipped. This is the same amount I've been nursing all afternoon, she thought, and they haven't noticed. No point in broadcasting that I can't drink much anymore.

"Joe told me that Richard said you're going to hire an— I don't know what he called it. Assistant? Aide? Someone to help with cooking and the kids and such."

"Wife?" Bea suggested.

The three of them laughed.

"But really, Mara, is that true? Because if so, I'm feeling terribly guilty having let you do all that work."

Mara twisted her glass, then glanced toward a window.

"Daylight topic, right?" she asked and Christy smiled.

"What's that?" Bea asked. "I like the sound of it."

"Something so scary you never discuss it at night," Christy explained. "So. True?"

"Sometime. Richard worries about my handling things when he's working long hours, so he's thought of buying a cellular phone, a panic button, a beeper, all sorts of gadgets. His newest idea is to hire a housekeeper to live here, take over the cleaning from the service we have, do most of the cooking, ferry the kids around and mostly watch out for me, in case I fall in the shower, that sort of thing."

"And is that okay with you?" Christy asked.

"Falling in the shower?"

"Don't get cute," Bea said.

Mara shrugged.

"I don't know. I don't think we're at that point yet. After all, I'm still driving off to work everyday."

"My brake pedal idea worked out?" Bea asked.

"Perfectly," Mara answered. I have to change the subject, she thought. Even in daylight, I get spooked by this, and I don't like being reminded of arguments, of Richard's face. I don't like the idea of learning to be watched over. That's not what I want right now. I'd rather concentrate on how to paint clouds or what to do about someone on my staff who's always late.

"Did Joe get that Spielberg movie Richard's been talking about?" she asked Christy.

Christy sank back in the rocker.

"Yeah. That will mean weekends, I'm afraid. You guys need more counselors at the Women's Clinic? I'll need something to do with myself. I know! How about if I apply for the nanny job, Mara?"

Bea shook a finger at Christy.

"Ever hear of work, my friend? You got any skills?"

"Let me think. I must have some," Christy said, scratching her head in an exaggerated effort. After a moment, she cried, "How about cleaning shower tile? I've even used a toothbrush on it."

"Toothbrush?" Mara said. "Are you sure you weren't nine months pregnant? Sounds like nesting to me."

They laughed, then sat quietly. Mara could hear birds, the sound of a lawnmower. How would it feel to hear the sound of someone cleaning her kitchen, bathing her kids? Perhaps answering her telephone to confirm, "Mara's fine. No spills today, sir."

Suddenly, Bea said, "I was reading Proverbs last night. Chapter 31. That's about the virtuous woman. Remember?"

Christy made a scoffing sound, but Bea continued.

"It's fascinating to see what men used to think a virtuous woman was. She clothed her family well and sold linen and kept a good house, 'eating not the bread of idleness.' And she got up in the early morning to make meat for her family and her maids."

"I liked how she dressed: 'in silk and purple," Mara said.

"And her husband and her children all respected her and had nothing but praise," Bea added.

"And in her tongue is the law of kindness," Mara quoted.

"She 'feareth the Lord and she shall be praised," Bea cried out, lifting her hands toward the ceiling.

"Stop!" Christy yelled. "This is insulting! Just add good sex and men still want the same things."

Bea shook her head, bright enamel earring loops flashing against her hair.

"No, I got a different take on it this time. I used to feel pissed off, just like you. But now, I think I almost envy that woman. Her life had a focus, you know? Her whole life was a temple to glorify God. The way she kept her house and kids and husband, his position in the town, it was all a temple. And that's all she wanted!" Bea turned to Mara.

"Don't you envy her? Wouldn't you like your life better if it had a focus?"

"Would I?" Mara wondered aloud. "Well, yes, having everything affirm my role, and having everyone sure of what that role is—yes, that would be easier."

"That's what I mean," Bea insisted. "The virtuous woman may have worked hard, but it was all designed for only one purpose. Everyone in her family and in the whole blasted town knew what her purpose was!" Bea fell back against the cushions. "Man! I envy her."

"But your life has meaning," Christy wailed. "You act like, without a single focus, everything you do is lessened, but that's not so. Mara! Think about it! What's the focus of your life? And you better not say God."

Mara shook her head. "Not God, Christy. I don't know. I've never thought about it."

"Well, I have," Bea said. "Maybe for only 24 hours, but that's something. And I've decided that my focus is *me*. Everything I do is because I want to, it pleases me. I eat, I teach, I buy clothes, I clean my house, all because I want to. That's awful!"

"But others are helped in the process," Christy argued. "Don't you think being virtuous made that woman happy?"

"That wasn't her goal," Bea said. "She wanted only to glorify God, honor Him, do whatever it took to show Him her devotion. Feeling good about it wasn't the point."

Christy turned to Mara.

"My focus is love, I think," Christy said.

Bea snorted, but Christy continued.

"I've never thought about it, but that word sums up the motivation for most everything I try to do, be it favors for Joe or decorating the house or meals or whatever. Your turn, Mara."

The two women stared at her, and Mara suddenly wished that a child would appear abruptly in the doorway, knee scraped or eyes wet. Where are interruptions when you need them?

"I hate to admit it," Mara said, "but I don't have any focus right now. Everything's changing. Meanwhile, I think my life is centered around MS."

Bea and Christy became still and serious.

"Coping with it affects everything I do all day," Mara continued. "But I try not to *focus* on it. Does that make sense? Can I have a center without a focus?"

Mara looked from one friend to the other. It was Bea who stood, glass in hand.

"I toast the seeker," she said. "Many daughters have done virtuously, but thou excellest them all."

"Well, now." Mara flushed.

Christy stood also.

"Here's to daylight topics," she said, lifting her glass. "May life's focus join the list."

"Here, here!" they all cried and drained the last of their champagne.

Scrapbook, page 24

Four items, contrasting sharply with one another, march in a row down this page.

First is a thank-you card. The ink drawing on the front is of an exhausted woman, holding a fire extinguisher in a messy kitchen. The drawing is black and white except for the woman's head, which is wrapped in a bright red bandanna. A skinny cat licks at something dripping from a burned pan, dishes overflow the sink, and several children either peer in the window or over the fence at a fire truck rushing from the corner of the card.

Inside, the message reads, OH. DID WE SAY THANK YOU? and it is signed by both Bea and Christy.

So they liked each other well enough to sign the same card. Pauline had been right about Mara's taste: the guests had enjoyed one another.

Next is a Catholic church program, serious in its listing of the sections of an apparently ordinary service—no famous speaker or guest organist. Did Mara choose church, feeling the need to buttress her determination? Or was it perhaps Richard, the powerless onlooker? And was this something they relied upon routinely, or was it the exploration of a single Sunday?

Below is a sheet of two-holed, lined paper containing a poem entitled LAMENT OF THE ARTHRITIC COOK.

> If I try to cook,
> I drop the spoon
> Which splashes its stuff
> Around the room
> And spills the pan
> Across the stovetop.

> Green goo seeping,
> This calls for my old mop.
> Rinsing the mop
> After clearing the sink,
> I bend toward the floor
> Where quick as a wink
> My hip cries out,
> The goo catches fire,
> The smoke alarm rings,
> And I curse the mire
> Of kitchen and knives
> Cutting boards and grater.
> I should call Meals on Wheels—
> It *has* to be safer.

Mara—[Pauline has written across the bottom]
It's not great literature, but I thought you'd appreciate my attempt.
Much love (and understanding)—P
On the bottom of the page, mounted on a trimmed index card, is a small ad cut neatly from the newspaper.
Live-in Attendant Wanted [the heading says]
For working mother with MS; needing light care. Mara 213-322-9805.
Drawn on the card in black marker is a frowning face followed by a note in Mara's writing: *Perhaps no one will call.*

In a way, this request for help is not for Mara; it is to ease Richard's mind. Perhaps he worries that he is working to pay for not being at home, an irony shared by all working parents, working children of the elderly, working spouses of the disabled. Perhaps the desire to pray is not Mara's either; it is to calm Richard's soul.

How much easier it would have been to carry the cross than to watch Jesus labor.

Chapter 21

Alone in her dining room, Mara watched the rain. She thought of the song by—was it the Mamas and the Papas?—about how it never rains in California, it pours, and that's the truth. No daily dusting of afternoon thunder and showers, cleaning the skyscrapers and the heavens. No, it hardly ever rains and when it does, torrents pour into dry washes, filling them to overflowing, washing away foundations, parked cars, power poles. I'm glad the kids and I are snug at home, glad it's Sunday, only sorry that Richard had to work.

Tomorrow evening is the first interview resulting from the ad, and I'm not looking forward to it, she admitted to herself. The woman sounded dull, no other way to describe it. Good enough to interview, but dull. She would cook and clean and drive and had been a nurse's aide in Colorado. Her sister had MS, so she knew what help was needed. In short, she met the requirements, except, Mara thought, the unspoken ones: interests, lively awareness, sense of humor. How can I tell someone I won't hire her because she has no sense of humor?

The kids should have a say, and maybe they'll give me some excuse. Maybe she won't like driving up here. Maybe between now and tomorrow, she'll fall and do something to her...sacroiliac. Face it, Mara thought, you don't want anybody. It isn't her character; it's the position itself.

The front door opened, startling Mara so that she twisted in her chair.

"Hi," Richard called out. "Don't everyone throw their arms around me at once," he hinted.

Only Mara greeted him.

"The kids are playing Nintendo," she explained, pulling back from his hug. "That you, Dad?" Matt called out from the den.

"Yes, but keep your distance. I'm all wet. Don't all of you rush out here. I'll tell you when I'm ready."

"Okay," Matt said, sounding distracted.

Richard shrugged out of his raincoat and hung it in the closet.

"What a day," he said. "We must have played this one section a hundred times."

Mara sat next to him on the couch, while he used a corner of his handkerchief to wipe his neck.

"What's Spielberg like? What's the movie like?"

"I couldn't even tell you. After awhile, we get so bleary, we don't care where we are or what we're doing. That's usually the cut the director likes."

Mara smiled.

"Christy calls that 'reaching the plateau.' All the stress is off because you've reached level playing ground. Speaking of level ground, Anne called today and she wants me to fly to Tennessee next month. We could drive around, see the Smokies, and she could get me a ticket for Pavarotti's recital. Can you believe it? Pavarotti in Knoxville? In the campus gym!"

Richard raised a hand to stop her.

"What's that have to do with a level field or whatever you said?"

"Pavarotti won't climb stairs. He has all kinds of requirements—certain foods and movies he wants in a certain kind of hotel room—and they'll have to install a ramp backstage so that he can walk through the curtain without climbing a step. Isn't that wild?"

"Anne can get tickets?"

Mara nodded. He looks so tired, she thought. I should stop chattering.

"She's bought hers already, and she'll get another one for me to keep Pauline company in easy access."

Richard straightened.

"I hadn't thought of that. Can you manage? With your suitcase and everything?"

"I've already figured out that I need a collapsible cane and a suitcase on wheels. With those two things, I should be in good shape."

Mara pushed back Richard's wet hair and kissed his cheek.

"I really want to do this. No telling how much longer I can travel alone. And that's why—" Mara took a deep breath "—I don't think we need an attendant just yet. If I can handle a trip across the country, I must still be okay."

Before Richard could answer, the three children and the dog rushed in, Kiki and Ken climbing onto Richard's lap, talking at once about the game and exactly how Matt had cheated. Mara reached out a hand to mess Matt's hair, but he ducked away from her and began defending himself in the loudest voice, and her efforts to quiet them failed.

"I hope you don't expect us to side with anyone in this mess," Mara grumbled, knowing that the subjects of Tennessee and an attendant were shelved for now.

Bea carefully tore open a second packet of sugar.

"I like the challenge," she explained to Mara who was sitting across from her in the cafeteria, watching intently. "If a package has a line or an arrow, my competitive nature comes out, and I try to follow it exactly."

Discarding the tidy edge of the package, Bea dumped the sugar and stirred.

"So, tell me: how did you convince Richard to drop the nanny idea?"

"By not making him drop it," Mara answered. "It never works to try to force him directly. He's helping me plan for the Tennessee trip, so we just quietly let the other slide. The only definite agreement I got out of him was to cancel the one interview I had scheduled."

"But the subject will come back at some later date."

"I'm afraid it has to." Mara stared into her coffee cup. "The doctor gave me a prescription for a walker."

"And?"

Mara heard her immediate response and felt relieved. I can never faze her—she's like Pauline that way. Buoyed by Bea's acceptance of what had been almost unspeakable, Mara gained energy.

"The walker's my next step. You know, this gradual deterioration is amazing—it really is. When I first needed a cane, I thought, 'Well, that's it now. By this time next year, I'll be in a wheelchair.' Instead, I discover how slow deterioration can be, and I'm constantly surprised by things I can't do anymore, like use chopsticks or hold my feet in those awful stirrups at the gynecologist's. I have to drink mineral water instead of wine coolers, and last week I discovered that I shouldn't order steamed rice on a hot day."

Bea looked surprised at that.

"I can't handle the warmth," Mara explained. "I just go limp, like cooked spaghetti."

"I prefer spaghetti to rice any day," Bea said.

"Thank you for your vote of confidence. Anyway, I should be glad it's been so gradual. Bowels, bladder, handwriting, eyesight—all falling apart by tiny increments. On one level, it's fascinating to watch."

"And on another level, it's the pits. Share a brownie. I don't want all this. Did I tell you I'm starting a diet?" Bea split the thick hunk of chocolate and nuts in half and pushed a plate across the table.

"I couldn't stand it, Mara," she said. "Let me lose an arm or break my back and I'll eventually accept my limitation. But this constant accommodation—" she shook her head emphatically—"that's not for me. I'm not that—tolerant, I guess it is."

"Tolerant?"

Bea nodded.

"It's a form of that. Fate is handing you these symptoms and you're accommodating them, folding them into your life."

"But that makes it sound like I could resist."

Mara remembered a pamphlet she'd seen on alternative medicine. She'd been sorry the Clinic was distributing it, because by the time she'd finished reading about endorphins, meditation and herbs, she could have believed that her illness was her own fault, and whatever is my own doing, she'd thought, is also within my power to cure. I believe in being my own doctor, but responsibility for bringing this on or getting rid of it is too much.

"Okay, then, call it patient. Stoic. Whatever it is, I'm not it!"

"I can't take any credit," Mara said. "That's just the way I am. Genetics, breeding, environment, whatever. I come from a line of hardy women."

"Your mother, too?"

"So skip her," Mara laughed. "All the rest are strong characters. I can't imagine Grandma throwing up her hands and taking to bed. I wasn't made that way, so don't admire me."

Mara finished her coffee. I hadn't known I feel that way, but I really do, she thought. Admire only the actions or traits which take effort, not the ones which come naturally. Those I'm not responsible for; I can only notice them with some wonderment.

Bea shook her head, grabbed the bill and stood.

"Accept admiration whenever it's offered," she said. "Now eat the rest of that brownie or I'll shove it down your throat."

"I always thought 'Song of Solomon' was longer," Pauline said during her Sunday telephone conversation. "It has such a reputation. Sort of a verbal *National Geographic*, if you know what I mean."

"The minister read from 'Song' at our wedding," Mara said, "but he quickly added some other passages so everyone would know we'd been properly married."

"I can't see how it fits," Pauline continued. "All this stuff praising her neck and belly and…other parts of a female's anatomy. Not very Biblical, it seems to me."

Mara couldn't hold her secret any more.

"I have a surprise for you."

"What's that?" Pauline asked. She's going to tell me— what?

"I'm coming to Knoxville, so you'd better clean up your bedroom before I get there."

Pauline shrieked, and for a few moments she and Mara talked over one another. Finally, Pauline's voice won out.

"You wouldn't believe how excited this town is about Pavarotti," she said. "Such a great name coming to little old us. And you'll be here to explain everything."

"Hardly, Pauline!"

"Well, you certainly know more about classical music than Anne and I do, and Fred's only going to keep us company. Who'll take care of the children?"

"I've hired an ex-student of mine, Rachel Reid. She'll be fine for a long weekend."

Those simple sentences hide a complicated story, Mara thought. How I helped Rachel decide to end her pregnancy, then lost her, then found her, then failed her with my advice and lost her again, then helped her re-enroll. But the bottom line is, she likes my kids, they like her and I trust her.

"I should have known," Pauline chuckled, "that you'd have everything under control."

That's my image, Mara thought after she hung up. The calm, collected, well-organized woman-on-the-move—who's suddenly stopped, lucky just to hang on to the position she has, never mind advancement. Can't risk a new job with new health insurance. Can't risk new supervisors who aren't sympathetic…

Stop it, she told herself. Make lunch and read the kids stories and do a load of wash and grab a nap and don't think about…it. Hands out to steady herself, Mara walked to the mirror in the hall and peered closely at her face. She saw freckles on her cheeks, a few wrinkles at the corners of her eyes, no gray yet in the long auburn hair. Still fairly youthful-looking, she thought, and smiled to herself. She'd read that MS seemed to slow the signs of aging—one of the few advantages—but only because people with the disease need to rest more.

"If we all napped every afternoon," the neurologist was quoted as saying genially, "we'd all look as good as you do."

Balancing self-consciously, Mara walked back to the breadboard and the row of sandwiches and carefully picked up the butcher knife. With his skill at napping, she thought, Grandpa would have looked eternally fit.

Scrapbook, page 25

At the top of this page, torn but taped together, as though thrown away and then salvaged, is a yellow telephone message with SKILLS CENTER printed on the top. The caller for Mara was a Dr. Erwin from the UCLA MS Research Clinic and the message reads:

Going out of town. Wanted you to know that your white count is still too low for the drug trial. He'll keep you informed of other experiments.
K

Below the message is a personal note from K:
Sorry—[she writes] *I know this was important to you.*

This message does not need the addition of a frowning face—the mended rip tells the story.

Below the message is a note from Matt, written in the stiff perfection of newly learned cursive.

Mom, [Matt writes]
This is an official invitation to play me in a doubel solatare game the winner gets to pick out the pizza and maybe desert.
Love XXOO Matt

Mara must have played cards with her children often enough that Matt felt the invitation would be welcome. Perhaps Mara was also eager to work crossword puzzles with them, to play Scrabble, to interest them in old radio shows or the humor of Victor Borge. These are the delights of those who are not fleet-of-foot, the sedentary, intellectual pursuits which such people come to love rather than spending lifetimes regretting what they cannot do.

Next to the invitation is a color photo of the two of them playing cards on the dining room table, cleared of dishes and pads, only soda glasses showing. In Matt's careful script is the caption: SOLATARE MARATHON. Both are grinning, fingers outspread to protect the center piles. They share a delight: this is something I can do, they are both thinking.

Following is a photo of Mara's children tossing a frisbee, their dog jumping below the arc of the toy. They are playing on the sand, surf rolling close to their feet, and their mouths are open in laughter and shouting. The photo is full of colors: the children's striped and spotted bathing suits, the black and white dog, the orange of the frisbee and the shiny blue metal roof of the apartment building behind them. From a window in that building a gray blur stands, indistinguishable except that a red arrow points to it. Written above the arrow are the words, THAT'S ME!, a wry acknowledgment that Mara is often a distant observer.

But the final item brings Mara into the action again. It is from a travel agent, confirming her flight to Knoxville. She leaves LAX on a Friday, changing to a small plane in Nashville, and arriving in Knoxville mid-afternoon, the trip being reversed the following Tuesday. Mara will travel a great distance to hear Pavarotti sing, but that is not really her reason for making the trip. This is an involvement. It is also an effort to prove—to Richard, to herself—that, relying on her own resources, she can still do.

IV

Rachel Reid

Chapter 22

When the flight attendant asked if she wanted a drink, Mara shook her head and turned to the window, staring into clouds.

She had packed and re-packed carefully for this trip, keeping her bag light while watching the daily temperatures in Knoxville, so that she could feel confident in omitting a coat. Into her shoulder bag had gone a paperback and her collapsible cane, and tucked carefully into a pocket of her suitcase was a pile of snapshots of her paintings. She had remembered to wrap some fresh avocados which Matt had picked from a neighbor's trees.

Mara hadn't traveled a great deal, but enough to know that this trip felt different. Partly it was going alone to visit friends—that seemed self-indulgent to a working mother. Partly it was proving to Richard and herself that she could still function safely, independently. And partly, it was watching herself in a new situation to see what she could and could not do. Grim fascination.

So when she stood, she noticed if she could walk down the aisle without touching seat backs; as she deplaned, she watched whether she needed to steady herself on the railings; as she hugged Anne, she was aware of leaning against the wall to provide extra support for her tight squeeze of Anne's shoulders; and as they reached the baggage claim area, she was suddenly very glad when her friend offered to claim and carry.

"Welcome!" Pauline shouted as Mara got out of the car at Anne's home. "How wonderful to be together!"

Mara hugged her, glad to feel Pauline's embrace, but as she toured Anne's house, then sat down for coffee, Mara felt peculiar: these familiar friends were in an unusual setting. Especially Pauline—here she wore soft wools instead of white hospital polyester, and she let Anne lead from room to room, ending at the kitchen table, instead of answering phone calls from friends wanting to chat, or sitting on her veranda, sipping coffee, surrounded by desert heat and aromas. Here she was a mother, living in a portion of her daughter's home and world.

"I'm making the best of it," Pauline said when Anne had left them to answer the telephone.

"You don't ever think you should have gone to your brother's, do you?"

Mara was surprised when Pauline didn't answer right away, when her face seemed to be hiding, not facing, some realization. Finally she said, "I love my daughter," and Mara knew that Pauline had doubts about the wisdom of her choice.

Before they could continue their conversation, Anne reappeared, and the topic wasn't mentioned again.

During the next two days, they slept late, ate leisurely meals and took brief sightseeing trips to the river, the university, a fair, the Smokies. On both days university basketball played on television, Anne and Mara talking over the announcers while Fred, instead of hushing them, kept moving his chair closer to the set so that he could catch the details of his favorite sport, and Pauline excused herself to bed. Mara watched the way Anne and Fred were with one another, comparing their tones of voice, their quickness to compromise, the pace of their days, with hers and Richard's, and then disliked herself for doing that. One comparison she would let herself make was that they spent more time together, which perhaps confirmed that an attendant for Mara *was* a reasonable idea, if only to provide company. That occurred to Mara one night as she was climbing into bed and she pushed the thought aside, saving it for daylight.

"You look great!" Anne said. Mara was wearing a black dress with long pearls ("These are called opera-length," Mara had announced. "Absolutely appropriate."). "I like that pattern on your stockings."

Mara looked at her feet in their soft-soled flats.

"With such a dull beginning down there, I try to liven up the legs a little."

"How about me? Do I look all right?" Anne asked. "Everyone seems to get more dressed up down here."

Mara smiled.

"I covet your shoes and the short skirt," she said. "I always feel slightly frumpy, especially with the cane."

Anne grabbed her purse.

"When Mother was recuperating from her hip operation," she said, "we had to go to a wedding and she was embarrassed about how casual her outfit was. But when she stood behind the walker, suddenly what she was wearing didn't matter. We agreed that when you use one of those things—and maybe this is true for canes, too—it isn't whether you're dressed right, it's whether you show up at all!"

Mara laughed and felt reassured.

"Just like when you're pregnant," she agreed. "I wore the same dress to any fancy occasion. Nobody expected much. It was sort of liberating, actually."

Anne nodded but said nothing, and Mara regretted mentioning pregnancy. Standing in the lobby of the university gym, waiting for Fred to park the car, Mara absorbed the excited voices around her. To be in the middle of a gala event, she thought, to see Fred hurrying through the glass doors, smoothing his hair, and know that he's looking for us—well, this is exciting and I'm glad I've come.

Fred spotted them. "Where's Pauline?" he asked, breathless. "I thought you were all staying together."

Anne took his arm.

"Don't worry, she's over there by the elevator. She saw a woman from church."

Fred shook his head.

"Church doesn't matter," he mumbled to Anne as they walked toward Pauline Mara felt confused, as though she'd arrived in the middle of a conversation.

"She keeps trying for buddies," Fred explained to Mara as they neared Pauline, "but it'll never happen because she wasn't born here. That makes all the difference."

"There they are!" Pauline cried, reaching for Anne's arm as the person next to her, a white-haired woman dressed in lavender and jewels, smiled politely. "My companions in culture! Charlotte, you know my daughter Anne and her husband Fred. And this is Mara, our wonderful friend from California, who claims she's come out here to see us, but we know the truth!"

"I've been found out," Mara laughed as she shook hands with the woman. "A Pavarotti groupie is all I really am."

Crowding into the elevator, they jockeyed with men in gray suits.

"I got you two seats on the mezzanine," Anne said, pulling four tickets from her purse. "We'll be on the other side and the next level up. Actually, I think you've got better seats."

"We deserve it," Mara said, taking the two tickets and grinning at Pauline.

"Do you want me to help you find your seats?" Anne asked as the elevator opened.

"Worry not," Mara said over her shoulder. "We'll do fine."

Pauline called, "Enjoy!" to Charlotte and then took Mara's arm, supporting her elbow.

"Who's helping whom here?" Mara laughed, but she liked the support, as they slowly approached the crowds. She noticed that people stepped aside for them, especially men, often gesturing with one arm, as though spreading a cape. Everyone is Pauline's age, Mara thought, yet I'm the one with a cane. Do we look peculiar?

"Goodness," Pauline said, "such a crowd. Well, I think that's wonderful. Now, where's our door?"

She stopped in confusion, reluctant to take unnecessary steps.

"Excuse me?" Mara called to a man wearing a satin ribbon on his lapel, "Could you help us?"

The man hurried over to them and looked at the tickets Mara extended.

"Well, ladies," he said with a soft, southern accent and a slight bow, "I think we can do better than that. Would you follow me?"

He strode ahead, looking back often as though to ensure that they were making it through the jostling throng.

I'll stand straight and walk firmly, Pauline thought. I certainly don't want to whine, and there's no point in being afraid. Mara will take care of me. No, I'll take care of her. Anyway, once I get through today, I'll be fine.

Stopping at a door, the man turned and smiled encouragingly.

"Here's where a number of our handicapped are sitting," he said, "and I think the seats are much better than the ones you bought. May I ask," he said, bowing toward Mara as they moved through the door, "what your affliction is?"

Despite the fact that the area he had led them to was seating off a short, steep flight of stairs, Mara felt his genuine concern. She tightened her hand around Pauline's elbow to keep her from taking a step and answered him calmly.

"Multiple sclerosis. The cane is my assistant."

The man clucked his tongue.

"I'm so sorry," he said. "Now, let me help you both with those stairs," and he led first one, then the other, down the flight to two large seats behind the railing. Mara noticed that the box contained two other couples occupying the four other extra-wide seats, both men gripping the tops of multiple-pronged canes, both women sitting sideways, adjusting their husband's coats and ties. We all look relieved, Mara thought as she folded her cane, and a little proud.

Pavarotti 's recital was grand theater. Mara relished every move with his handkerchief, every gesture toward individuals on the ground floor—"They're our wealthiest townsfolk," Pauline whispered. "Those tickets cost a bundle, but you get to go to a reception afterwards." She patted Mara's hand with mock sorrow. "I'm awfully sorry we didn't have enough money."

Always enjoying a live recital, Mara leaned forward, enraptured. She thought suddenly of Mrs. D. and how she' would have loved to hear Mara's description of this event. She'd feel responsible for having exposed me to this bit of Culture. But honestly, she'd care more about his singing than the other details of the evening. She really did value serious appreciation of the arts.

Which is why, when the auditorium filled with the smell of buttered popcorn during intermission, Mara groaned. For the sake of Mrs. D., let alone Pavarotti, she wanted the people of Knoxville to acquit themselves graciously. It apparently wasn't going to happen.

"Did you want something to eat?" Pauline asked, turning her knees so that Mara could get by if she answered yes.

"No, thanks." Mara stretched toward the couple behind her. The woman was twisting in her seat, patting her husband's hand and looking around nervously.

"Did you need some help?" Mara offered, but the woman shook her head.

"I think I'll just stay here," she said, leaning forward. "There's no point in struggling through the crowds. This is our first trip out since his stroke," she whispered, "and I don't want to try too much."

Mara thought how pretty she looked, making an effort.

"I like your necklace," Mara said. "Is that turquoise?"

Blushing slightly, the woman touched the silver chain around her neck and nodded.

"It's lovely, isn't it? My daughter sent it to me last Christmas, but this is the first chance I've had to wear it."

Mara liked the Tennessee accent, very soft and—genteel. Did Pavarotti have time to notice such things?

As the lights dimmed, Mara waved a quick goodbye to the couple behind her, and Pauline smiled at the other woman who sat proudly, holding her sleeping husband's hand. Mara felt linked with the people in this box in a way she hadn't felt since she'd led the MS Support Group. We're all struggling, she thought, and we have to take care of each other, even if all we can do is to offer sympathy.

Afthe second half, the encores began, the audience yelling out titles, Pavarotti re-singing some of the arias he'd already sung on his program. He made a joke about never having performed in a theater with such a strong smell of popcorn, and the audience laughed proudly. Pauline began to gather her jacket and purse.

"Sit still," Mara whispered.

"It's not over?"

"Look at the orchestra. They're arranging their scores. If I had binoculars, I could tell you what he'll sing next."

When Pavarotti again stepped from behind the curtain, Pauline squeezed Mara's hand.

"You're so smart," she whispered.

Finally, it ended, Pavarotti remaining behind the heavy curtain. The same usher re-appeared to help each of the six of them up the stairs, where they stood for a moment, canes wobbling but smiles broad, and they wished one another a pleasant evening, a safe journey home. The usher led Pauline and Mara to the elevator, and they emerged a few moments later to wait by the doors until Anne and Fred caught up with them.

During the ride back to Anne's, Pauline knew she was babbling like a teenager: about the popcorn and Pavarotti's voice and what good seats they had and how smart Mara was. I sound silly, Pauline thought, but I can't help it. I'm so happy. Never mind the Bible before I go to bed; next is Isaiah and he just won't fit.

Watching the stiff backs of her hosts, Mara felt increasingly convinced that they'd not enjoyed the concert nearly as much as she and Pauline had. It was something of a personal triumph for both of us, she thought, whereas Anne and Fred hadn't connected with anyone around them. From the sound of it, they'd worried so much about Pauline and Mara's comfort that they couldn't enjoy the concert.

Well, that was nice of them, Mara thought as she smoothed the program flat against the bottom of her suitcase, but it was wasted energy. They would have done better to spend their time really trying to enjoy themselves. Somehow, the desire to participate in pleasant experiences is intensified for me now.

Compensation, she thought. Could that be happening here?

Scrapbook, page 26

On this page is only one item, the program of Pavarotti's concert torn from a thicker book. The list of his arias exists as a reminder of beautiful music. It is also a reminder of the entire trip: sightseeing in the Great Smokies, eating roasted potatoes, shopping, fingering carved Santas, tapping a foot to Country Western songs. Pavarotti's program represents a weekend which was more than classical and which could not be enjoyed in a tuxedo or while waving a silk cloth. But no matter how limited its focus, the program will always return the uplifting memory of being connected.

Scrapbook, page 27

The next page is filled with slips of paper, most of them City College Skills Center telephone messages.

Tues., 2
M—
Chuck Winzen called from Pinecrest. Prob w/ permits. Call him. (209) 443-9028. Leave message. Sounds anxious.
    K
Below that is taped a second:
Mon., 10
M—
Chuck called. Permits ok! Start foundation Wed. No return call needed.
    K.
Then a third:
M—
Chuck called. Surprise snow storm. Everyone advises waiting on foundation until summer. Call him. (209) 443-9028. Leave message. Sounds disappointed. (Isn't this what you predicted?!)
    K
And a fourth:
Thurs., 11
M—
Chuck again! Framing nearly finished. Have you selected appliances from the catalogues he sent? Carpenter needs specs. (209) 443-9028. Sounds eager.
    K
Followed by a fifth:
Tues., 2

M—

Chuck, of course. Big prob, maybe delay: metal for roof lost in Stockton. No need to call, just wanted to let you know.

K

Then a piece of notepaper, taped on all four sides:

M—[Richard writes]

I want to let you know officially IN WRITING that we are never doing this again. No additions, no new houses, no selling and buying, nothing. If I ever see another bank form or construction contract, I'll scream first, take a stiff drink next and then run away and hide. With my clarinet. You may never see me again.

Love,

The man who makes too much—but not quite enough

Then a snapshot of six people squinting against summer sun in a vivid blue sky. Behind the group is a modern home, shingles around dramatic windows. Mara and Richard stand seriously behind their three children and a short, slender young woman. In Richard's hand is a checkbook, in Mara's a pen, both held out toward the camera.

Mara's lettering below says PINECREST—FINALLY!

Having bought a piece of paradise, they have built their retreat. They have grasped the ideal. Do they look apprehensive? No, only broke.

Carol Huebner

Rachel Reid

Chapter 23

Rachel sat on the floor in the twins' bedroom—Marika had corrected her when she'd referred to it as Ken's room—and pulled apart a Lego truck. Its doors were needed for a building she and the children were constructing, a colorful, tall, wobbly structure with turrets and windows and every door they could find.

"There!" Kiki announced proudly as she snapped the final door between two columns. "I did it!"

"*We* did it," Matt corrected, surveying the huge building. "Now we can put in the animals," and he began adding tiny creatures which Ken had been quietly assembling.

Kiki reached out to grab Matt's arm.

"Don't put it there!": she screamed. "Ken doesn't want it there!"

Matt slapped her hand, Kiki slapped him back, Ken reached in to rescue his animals, which had begun to break apart, and Rachel thought, Good grief, will they hurt each other? Trying to rescue and to calm, she distracted them by pulling up a fire truck, and they forgot the animals. Rachel sat back and watched them.

Twenty years ago, she remembered, I tried to play with Pete, but, being older, he bossed me around all the time so it was no fun. I was always crying or running away to hide. These kids at least tough it out with each other. But she smiled, thinking of her older brother. Even though he took seriously being the man of the house, making big decisions, giving Mama advice, he went off to serve in the Marines— *for life*, he had announced proudly. That left me alone with a woman who hadn't shared her bed in years and didn't like talking about—all the things Rachel had wanted to know.

The front door banged and the three children dropped their toys and ran for the living room. When Rachel caught up with them, they were pulling at Mara's coat and talking at once.

"Sorry," Rachel laughed. "Not much of a restful homecoming."

Steadying herself against the backs of chairs, Mara made her way to the couch without her cane. This lunging must look awful, she thought, and resolved to try her cane at home the next time the place was empty.

"Don't worry about restful," she laughed. "If I'd wanted that, I shouldn't have had three kids."

The telephone rang and Rachel went into the kitchen to answer, listening for a moment before calling into the living room.

"Melissa and Terry wonder if you guys could come over to play until dinner."

Three pairs of eyes turned to Mara.

"What do you think, Rachel?" Mara asked in mock seriousness. "Should we let them out of our sight?"

Rachel pretended to be carefully considering a weighty question.

"I could walk up there with them," she offered. "Then, when they're ready to come home..."

"Yea! We can go!" the children screamed and ran for some toys to take along.

After they left and the house was quiet, Rachel and Mara shared a pot of tea in the dining room, sunlight filtering through the branches of eucalyptus trees.

Mara carefully stirred two sugar cubes, then looked up.

"Do I smell dinner?" When Rachel nodded, she said, "Wonderful. Did you use to cook for your mom?"

"Some, but cooking was something Mama liked to do for herself."

"So you just learned by watching. You don't talk much about your mom, Rachel. Was she a happy person?"

That's an interesting question, Rachel thought. Happiness as a measure.

"She was quiet," Rachel answered, "but contented enough. It didn't take much."

She must have believed that no hope means no despair, Mara thought. I've never been able to live that way.

"How old were you when your dad left?"

"Just a baby. I don't even remember him."

"Did your mother work? What did you live on?"

"Air!" Rachel laughed. "Mama cleaned houses and Pete got good jobs, most of them in construction, so that was a big help. After he went into the Marines, he used to send us a check."

"Sounds like a nice guy."

"He was. Is."

Mara poured more tea for both of them.

"Do you see him often?"

Rachel remembered when Pete was based in Georgia. That was horrible, his being so far away.

"He's near San Diego, so we can talk on the phone. All those years we lived in the same house, I never appreciated him, but now I do."

Maybe I shouldn't bring this up, Mara thought, but after all, this woman may help me shower, so we'd better be honest with each other.

"Was Pete involved in your pregnancy?" she asked. "Could you talk to him about the decisions you had to make?"

Rachel shook her head and stared at the plate if cookies. That was such an awful time, she thought. It still hurts to remember.

"He said he didn't like Christian's type," she answered. "In those days Pete thought anyone who smoked dope or read a lot of poetry was a communist. I'd told him how I'd met Christian at the library, when he was reading exactly the book I was looking for, and he'd decided the guy ought to be working, not reading."

"Libraries were suspicious places," Mara laughed.

"Exactly. Pete was happy on a missile range, Christian loved libraries."

There he was, Rachel remembered, sitting cross-legged on the floor, leaning against shelves of books, mouthing the words and moving his body slightly, as though conducting the poem. Beautiful, to see someone give himself so completely.

Then he walked me to a nearby coffeehouse, where he jumped onto a table and recited a chunk of "Kublai Kahn." Then he drove to the beach. He said all the right things to reassure me that we were kindred spirits about to have a transcendent experience, and I let him go on.

"How long were you together?"

"About six months."

"And then?"

And then. Finally having a boyfriend had felt wonderful, Rachel remembered. I even decided that Mama was missing out: there *was* such a thing as happiness, love—other than for one's children. Even college seemed less important, now that I had something else to fill my thoughts: Christian's views, his tastes. I wanted him to tell me what colors I should wear, what books I should read. It was wonderful having someone care enough to mold me.

"And then I got scared. I told Pete that I'd missed my period before I told Mama. Pete was furious—at everyone, it seemed. At me for letting some bum have his way with me, at Mama for not giving me more sense. And at Christian, obviously. Anyway, he knew exactly what I should do."

"Break up, of course."

"First. Then get an abortion. Then join the Marines."

"The Marines?" Mara cried. It's impossible to imagine Rachel crawling through wire holding a rifle, she thought.

Rachel nodded, flushing slightly.

"Bea helped me figure out that I wouldn't be happy." What she'd actually said, Rachel remembered, was that mystical experiences with daffodils don't happen on tanks. We'd both laughed at the time, but the image really stuck.

"You two were terrific," Rachel continued. "That whole situation at least served some decent purpose. Not at first, but eventually I came out of it all with a real determination to take charge of my life and make plans for myself. I don't think I ever thanked you for that."

Mara smiled at this beautiful young woman sitting across from her. Do I tolerate an attendant, she wondered ruefully, because I feel like I'm helping out the needy? That sounds like Mrs. D. doing her part for the coloreds. Oh well. Maybe we should judge the outcome without looking at the motivation. Lucy had a good job. Rachel's happy, she likes school, the kids and Richard and I love having her around. How we all arrived at this point is perhaps not as important.

"You thank me every time you make dinner," Mara said. "Anyway, you said something nice to both Bea and me after you re-enrolled."

"I should never have dropped out," Rachel mumbled. "But Mama was dying and I wanted to be with her. Then at her funeral I suddenly wondered if anyone would care about *my* death. That was scary. A few weeks later Pete called to tell me that a friend of his in Arizona had been best man at the wedding of a fellow named Christian, some fellow who planned to build a time travel capsule. It sounded like the same communist bum to him, and he gave me a lecture about how I was better off without him in my life. And I was."

Rachel shook her head and set down her empty teacup.

"By contrast with Christian's, my brother's life had such..."

"Order?" Mara suggested.

"Purpose," Rachel said. "I liked that and I wanted to quit floating."

"And then Richard called."

Rachel stood to clear the dishes.

"He told me I could read poetry aloud while you shower."

Mara laughed.

"He knew what would appeal to you."

Rachel carried the plates and cups carefully, setting them on the kitchen counter. He also pleaded with me to be there for you, Rachel thought, which really got me. Then he and Mara sent the long-stemmed rose and I thought, this was meant to be. Life is beginning to take shape. If I keep my eyes open and watch carefully, I can learn how it's done…whatever it is.

"I'd vote for Ramirez, don't you think?" Sitting on the living room couch, Mara leafed through the candidates' statements until she found his. "He has the experience, and maybe his ethnicity makes him more sensitive to the community. Anyway, I like the phrase "thieving politicos.' He'll never win but I'll vote for him."

Rachel held the pointer over the cardboard ballot.

"It's Ramirez, then?"

"Poke his hole," Mara said. "Is that it now?"

Rachel put aside the absentee ballot and looked through the guide.

"What about all the bond measures?" she asked.

Mara frowned.

"Any for parks or libraries?"

Skimming the pages, Rachel shook her head.

"Mostly prisons and roads," she said.

"Forget it. We're done."

Mara stuffed the ballot into its gray folder, then sealed the whole thing into a white City envelope, signing across the back as steadily as she could. As though people care enough about voting to cheat, she thought. I wish.

"If you give me that, I think I can still beat the mail truck," Rachel said, grabbing the envelope and hurrying for a stamp and the front door.

"Make it?" Mara asked as Rachel returned.

"Just. Here's the mail." Rachel sorted it into five piles: junk, Richard's stuff, Mara's stuff, Richard and Mara's stuff, and her own. They each tore and read.

"Bills," Mara said. "Nothing interesting. How about you?"

Rachel sank back against the couch cushions, hand covering her eyes. "Rachel?"

I can't believe it, she thought.

"Are you okay?" Mara asked.

Uncovering her eyes, Rachel looked at the letter in her lap.

"This is from Pete. Christian was killed."

"Killed? How?"

"On a trip to Sedona, he got drunk at a friend's. Crashed into a truck." Rachel buried her face in her hands. "The father of the baby I never had."

Mara reached out to pull her closer and rub her shoulder. Where are the words, she wondered, and said nothing. When Rachel looked up, her eyes were red and her cheeks were damp.

"A chapter ends. That's two chapters in one year—Christian and Mama—both ended."

"I'm sorry."

The two women sat quietly for a few moments before Rachel turned to face Mara.

"Does this sound horrible? If Mama and Christian were still around, this job and college couldn't have happened. It's as though I needed to have space for something new."

Mara smiled.

"Matt always used to point to a place on the right side of his tummy and say that he was completely full except for this one spot which needed dessert."

Rachel nodded.

"That's what I have—a space to fill."

"And the other letter? It looks official."

Rachel picked up the legal envelope.

"Very official. I got in, Mara. Cal State LA has accepted me!"

"Congratulations!" Mara cried as they hugged. "What major?"

The number of hours I've spent worrying about that, Rachel thought. I even went to a career counselor, took a bunch of tests. But I did it myself. I didn't run crying for someone to take over the decision.

"What made you hire me?" Rachel asked, delaying her answer.

"You had an interesting past—"

"—checkered."

"Sort of. Okay. And potential. And you needed a home, and your hours could be flexible, and you could go up to Pinecrest with me, and we all trust you. Do you want more?"

Mara remembered that when Richard had suggested Rachel, she had been frightened. Rachel was such a good choice that excuses were useless.

"Trust," Rachel said. "I never quite trusted Christian. That's a big part of why I didn't have his baby. Trust is important, I guess."

"It's almost everything," Mara answered. "I trust Richard, and then I worry about trusting him so much."

"You ought to feel blessed."

"You mean because he could have left me for some fair and nimble young thing? I do appreciate that. And yet, somewhere inside is the sense that I'm unworthy of my husband's loyalty. Why should anyone stick with me? I ask myself. Anyway," Mara said, "I don't know how we got onto that. Tell me your major."

Rachel looked from Mara to the ceiling. She was enjoying the suspense, letting it stretch, which was a novelty for her, and she marveled at how much she was changing. Would Mama be proud? No, probably scared. Would Christian like the new Rachel? More to the point, she thought, would the new Rachel have liked him?

"One day I put together all that I care about, and I came up with English. Maybe teach, maybe law school, certainly do some writing." She turned toward Mara. "What do you think?"

"Wonderful. Exactly right," Mara said. Then, taking a deep breath, she asked, "And can you stay with us while you go to Cal State?"

How far I've come, Mara thought, from not wanting any assistant at all.

Rachel looked at Mara directly.

"Of course I'll stay, unless I'm not still all those things which first attracted you."

"Every one of them," Mara said, "and more."

I can see relief all over her face, Rachel thought. I wonder if it shows on mine?

Scrapbook, page 28

Centered on this page are two graduation programs, one for Rachel receiving her AA degree, one for Matt going on to high school. Neither is listed as valedictorian; neither appears on the program performing some special function. Rachel's program is distinguished by a very long list of graduates in print so small that only a loved one could care. Matt's program, on the other hand, announces that it is an art school—from the modernistic design on the cover to the music staffs and theater masks floating on every page. Names of the graduating eighth graders take only a small amount of room—the class is not large.

So a milestone has been reached and passed by both of them, and they now proceed to new adventures, new aches. Occasionally, they may long for childhood, when they made so little effort, or for the plateau, where—they will mistakenly believe—an adult floats smoothly as a result of earlier diligence. Certainly life must become easier, they will think. If I only do well in those classes and obtain this degree, I'll get a job, rent an apartment, and quietly report to work each day, making no waves, bearing no disappointments. Certainly, that is what the future holds, does it not?

On the bottom is a newspaper photograph of a table full of people dressed up at an AIDS benefit. Centered are the faces of Mara and Richard, smiling up at someone who is stopping by their table, hand on the back of Mara's chair. The photograph is interesting for several reasons: one, because Mara and Richard are significant enough to be worth featuring at such an event; two, because Mara is identified in the caption as an "administrator/artist," which must mean that she pursues both equally; and three, because of what Mara is wearing: a dramatic velvet dress, cut low, which emphasizes a pearl and emerald necklace.

Perhaps she has never before worn that piece of jewelry, because the event was never appropriate for a dress, which would do justice to the jewels. Would she prefer wearing it as a joke with a muumuu? No, times have changed. She and Richard have changed. Now he is dressed in a tuxedo, a narrow velvet ribbon tying back his hair, and Mara is at ease with elegance. From this plateau, they must climb even higher.

Chapter 24

Mara passed the letter to Rachel, who read it carefully, then handed it back.

"Congratulations!"

"Thanks. I don't know if I'll go, though."

Rachel was surprised: it seemed like this couple did everything.

"Why not?"

Mara glanced over the letter again.

"San Jose…I don't know. It may be more than I want to mess with, using the walker in the airport and all that."

Pride, Rachel thought. Always respect another's pride.

"What if I go along?" she suggested. "Sort of casually, nothing obvious. I could even make the arrangements, if you'd like."

"Even so…"

"It might make you feel really terrific, to accomplish that. And you'd be giving the Skills Center some well-deserved publicity."

Mara smiled.

"Are you sure you aren't studying psych?"

"So let's go," Rachel said and moved toward the telephone.

"Well, now…"

The flight was uneventful. Since the plane was nearly empty, flight attendants gave away extra packets of nuts and were waiting with refills on drinks. Mara asked Rachel to catch her up on life at the university and described some of her own college days, making a conscious effort to be a good listener and not dominate the conversation—although she and Richard had noticed that Rachel was becoming, in her still soft-spoken manner, much more assertive. She had even begun quoting one of her favorite poets, Shelley, especially the lines, 'To love and bear; to hope till Hope creates/From its own wreck the thing it contemplates.'

"I'm loving and bearing," Mara joked, as the plane began its descent.

"Let's hope we don't have any wreck to create from," Rachel laughed, and they snapped their seat belts.

Once on the ground Rachel rented a wheelchair before Mara could protest, and they whisked through the terminal, piling baggage and Mara's walker onto her lap as she sat in the chair.

"You call this easy-access?" Mara mocked from behind the tower on her lap.

Rachel drove the rental car and within a few minutes they were at the hotel which, according to its marquee, was hosting the ACCA convention.

"Arthritic Counselors Convene Annually?" Mara joked.

"American Congenial Concubines Association?" Rachel offered.

"Welcome to the tenth annual convention of the Association of Community College Administrators!" The woman staffing the registration desk smiled broadly as she avoided looking at Mara's walker. "And your name?"

Rachel stuffed Mara's registration materials into her shoulder bag, pinned Mara's nametag onto her blouse and picked up their housing assignment, a special room with wide doors, low counters and plenty of wall bars. After she and Rachel unpacked, Mara sat at the small round table in their room to study the conference program.

"Here I am," she announced, and Rachel came to look over her shoulder. "Enabling Success: Panelists Describe Community College Efforts.' Three o'clock this afternoon in the Sierra Room. Which reminds me: when's your school out for Thanksgiving?"

"Not until that Wednesday afternoon. Did you want to have the turkey at Pinecrest?"

"It would be great, but I don't want to mess up your classes. I mean—" here Mara put on a pompous accent—"I do stress education above all things."

Rachel shrugged.

"One day won't make much difference. I can get work from the profs—they're all pretty nice guys." I don't sound like a little schoolgirl anymore, Rachel thought, and was pleased. "What about the kids?"

"Matt's going to Greg's house in New Mexico, which should be interesting for him. Sob. I'll have to go on bended knee to get Kiki and Ken out of school for the day. Kiki's not exactly their favorite person."

"More unruly behavior?"

Mara sighed, folded the convention program and looked up.

"You're a smart woman, Rachel. Isn't there something she could chant for attitude adjustment? Something which would make all her teachers love her?"

"But would you like it? I mean, if she were very different—"

"We'd feel a mixture of loss and relief. Right now, mostly relief."

Mara pulled papers toward her and Rachel slid her sweater from the back of the chair.

"You probably want to prepare, and I'd like to drive around for awhile. I've never been up here. Is that okay? I'll be back around 2."

"Make it 2:30. Even 4:00. You don't need to heckle me, although such an idea probably never occurred to you."

"Never. I'll see you at 2."

Rachel enjoyed driving—it was a kind of power which didn't frighten her—and she set off with a simple map provided by the rental agency. It was pleasant avoiding families of bicyclists, straggling in long lines around corners. Pulling onto a turnout, she got out of the car to stand on the edge of the road. This is so different from LA, she thought: a distinct town, for one thing, surrounded by low hills covered with dry grasses and oak trees. Down there is Stanford: if I drive close by, I wonder if I'll discover that it's a mirage.

Returning to San Jose, she parked near a restaurant which had outdoor tables and took a seat, pushing down on her hat to prevent the warm wind from whipping it off her head. People on the sidewalks move slowly, she thought, not pressured by deadlines on a weekend.

Watching the waiter disappear into the café after bringing her iced tea, she thought how cute he was, then realized that she hadn't noticed *that* for ages. 'Nothing in the world is single,' she smiled, warmed by the sun and the thought, and she stirred her drink.

Left alone, Mara tried to concentrate on her presentation, but she had already gone over her material carefully at home. The handout would remind her of everything, she was certain, so, planning to wander through the exhibits and arrive early at the Sierra Room, she began to dress. She had deliberately packed a dramatic outfit: a long teal green skirt and jacket with a coral blouse, patterned stockings and ankle-high boots. Splashy, she said to herself as she tied a bright scarf around her waist. She wanted to attract attention, she admitted that to herself, to surprise people who looked anxiously at the pusher of the walker.

It didn't take her long to discover that, without Rachel's shoulder bag, going to publishers' exhibits was useless—she couldn't carry enough in her purse—so she went on to her conference room, one quarter of a ballroom, fronted by a lectern and a long table with two microphones. Someone was already there, a woman whose name Mara couldn't read, wearing the ribbon of a convention official.

"I'm so glad you're early, Mrs. Leeds," the lady said as she pumped Mara's hand. "That dreadful fog has stopped a car *full* of presenters from the San Joaquin Valley and from Monterey as well. So you'll be the only one!"

"The only panelist?" Mara repeated, dumbfounded.

"I'll stay and introduce you myself—I feel somehow responsible for the fog." The woman's carefully blackened eyebrows curved in sorrow.

"How many people do you expect in the audience?" Mara asked, brain already reviewing her materials and imagining how long she could stretch her remarks.

"Oh, maybe 25 or 30. I know you'll do fine."

But the audience numbered closer to 100. Even after the woman made her explanations, no one left. In fact, after all the copies of Mara's handout had been distributed and she had begun to speak, more people crept in, whispering anxiously at the doorway, perhaps disappearing for a moment but reappearing with a chair in tow.

Not attempting to hide the walker waiting at the end of the table, Mara spoke: about what she called academic safety nets, about student expectations, about the true nature of needed remediation—not grammar drills or arithmetic worksheets. Knowing that she didn't need to share her presentation with anyone, she let herself elaborate with detailed examples, some humorous, some poignant, and ample personal philosophy, most of which she'd never expressed before but which she felt deeply. Spotting Rachel, she called on her to answer several questions.

When the workshop was over, the audience rose in applause. Mara was stunned.

"You were *wonderful!*" the conference official exclaimed, waiting until after the last person had shaken Mara's hand or left a business card. "Do you do this often?"

Mara began gathering the cards and slips of paper, hands trembling slightly.

"This was my first," she admitted.

"I can guarantee it won't be your last!" the woman said, shaking her hand again. "Your eloquence is very persuasive."

Mara thanked her, thanked anyone who was waiting to make one last comment, thanked those who helped her from the table. Rachel scooped the pile of papers into her shoulder bag, put a steadying hand under Mara's elbow, and together they walked back to their room.

"How did you do that?" Rachel asked.

Mara laughed, equally surprised.

"I don't know. It must have been Grandma speaking through me," she said.

"I just gave up," Pauline said into the telephone. "A whole row of nice names—Jeremiah, Hosea, Obadiah—but I couldn't get into those books. Somewhere around Joel I called it quits. Do you think God cares? Will He hold it against me?"

"You've read more than most people have," Mara assured her, "so I'm sure He'll give you extra-credit."

"I read further than Jerry did, I know that. He never talked about anything past Ecclesiastes."

"To every thing there is a season, and a time to every purpose under the heaven."

"That's the best part," Pauline said. "If the other books were like that, I'd still be reading them. Instead, they're full of death and treachery, and I got sick of it. So now you know what I'm going to do?"

Always a next step, Mara thought.

"What's that?"

"Just as soon as I'm in rehabilitation, I'm going to start The New Testament. It's not such wonderful writing, I guess, but I'm a lot more interested in the life of Jesus than the views of—of Zechariah."

This is typical of her, Mara thought: dropping a bombshell in a dependent clause.

"Rehabilitation?" Mara demanded.

"It's nothing," Pauline said, dismissing the topic. "Just a minor tune-up for my hip. I'll be up and around in no time. Anne wants to rent me a walker again, but I won't need it."

"Come on, Pauline, I use mine! It started off locked in my trunk, but now it's the only way I can get around. If it helps you, you should use it and be chipper." For the millionth time, am I telling her or myself?

"You sound like my daughter," Pauline said, and Mara couldn't tell if that was okay.

"How *is* Anne? As usual, I haven't heard from her in ages."

"She's terribly busy, what with her advertising job during the day and now teaching adults in the evenings. And Fred's started traveling all the time. I don't know. I wouldn't want their life. They make the best of it and I do admire them, but I'm glad Jerry and I had the marriage we did. And your brood? You've told me about San Jose, and of course I was sure you'd be splendid. Now tell me how Matt's doing."

"Every so often he sounds a little homesick."

"He's only fourteen, after all."

"We talk him through it. During the day he loves his school and wouldn't trade living away from home for anything. The twins were put in different classes this year and I'm glad. Kiki's too domineering."

"They need a chance to grow into separate people."

"Kiki asked her teacher how you know what evil is, and the teacher said that was a religious topic. End of discussion. Kiki's a real handful."

"We wouldn't want it any other way."

"Richard's been working weekends lately, but that should end soon, and then he says we'll go to Pinecrest, just the two of us."

"What a thoughtful man. Do you plan to keep him?" Pauline teased.

"Definitely," Mara answered. "Anyway, I think his warranty has expired. By the way, you would have loved the party the twins and I threw for Rachel. Ken made the banner. It said, 'Happy six moths in our house'! Did I tell you that Rachel's doing A-work at Cal State?"

"They've gotten a peach."

She's like our own grandma, Mara thought. No matter what we've done, she'll back us.

"And you?" Pauline asked. "How are you doing physically?"

"Crappy, thank you."

"That's a word I would never use, but I like hearing it. I know just how you feel. I try so hard to be brave that I get sick of myself."

Mara sympathized. They discussed Pauline's arthritis aches and Mara's new symptoms, promised to compare notes on the New Testament, sent love to everyone, and said goodbye.

After they hung up, both decided to call sooner than some Sunday in the next month—"because I do enjoy talking with her," they each thought.

After giving Ken a quick kiss where he sat drawing, Rachel lounged on the couch and began flipping through an old *People* magazine. Most of these folks are rich, she thought, and most of them are miserable. Does money have to go along with unhappiness? Give me a bundle and let me find out first-hand.

Pete and his wife are living on Marines pay, which probably isn't much, but he's happy. In his last letter he told me I should go visit our cousin in Idaho, that there are some beautiful lakes and forests up that way, but we have Pinecrest. Mama would be so happy to see me a junior in college. She always counted on me to be the first one in our family to walk across that stage and move the tassel to the other side. I tried telling her that it was no different than the tassel I had on my high school mortarboard, but she didn't believe me. College tassels are different, she said. They're more expensive. Well, she had a point.

Ken sat next to Rachel on the sofa and opened his book, glancing at Rachel's magazine to be sure that he was reading the way she did, and she looped an arm over his shoulder.

"See that motorcycle?" she asked, pointing to a picture in her magazine. "I had a friend who rode one."

Ken studied the picture.

"Where is he, your friend?"

"He died in a terrible accident. All his life he drove fast and recited poetry and drank."

"Why?"

"I…I'm not sure. I guess he had no ambition."

"What's that?"

"No direction. Nothing he wanted to accomplish."

"Whatddya mean?"

Rachel shook her head and turned the page. He'd never understand, she thought, about not having a goal. You learn to drift from your parents and your friends, so these kids'll probably never know how it's done.

Rachel closed the magazine, leaned her head against the back of the couch and stared at the ceiling.

I'm ready to write now, she thought. I've been waiting a long time, but I'm ready now.

Scrapbook, page 29

This is the final page in a book swollen by its many items, ripping from its once neat binding.

On the top is a clipping carefully cut from the campus newspaper, describing Mara's convention presentation. The article includes no picture, but the prose uses words such as "thoughtful" and "sensitive," so that an imagined smiling Mara can easily be added to the article.

Below it is a florist's card.
Standing applause from me, too.
Love,
R

Next are two contrasting items: a yellow telephone message from Kiki's counselor—
Please call Miss Grant ASAP. Teacher complaint that Kiki is an "iconoclast." (Where in the world could she have picked up that trait?)
K

—and a copy of a clarinet recital program with MATHEW LEEDS in fancy scroll on the front. On the bottom he has written *I did pretty well. Everyone liked it.*

Finally, a coffee-stained page with the heading, NEW YEAR'S RESOLUTIONS [in Mara's writing]:

1. *Cut down on coffee.*
2. *Cut down on coke.*
3. *Increase daily mileage on cycle.*
4. *Begin reading New Testament.*
5. *Hold more frequent staff meetings.*
6. *Take Kiki to see Father Michaels.*
7. *Tell* everyone *how much they mean to me.*

8. *Host poetry readings and music recitals.*
9. *Paint regularly.*
10 *Make fewer—what Ken used to call Revolutions—next year.*

The scrapbook ends. Perhaps it is only Volume One because certainly Mara's life continues. New pages would show grand events and tragedies, small achievements and setbacks.

After all, for Mara, for everyone, the Revolutions continue.

Epilogue

The tiny sandwiches Rachel had prepared and the tray of tea cookies and slices of pound cake sat on the shining coffee table, flanking the silver tray with its tea pot and two small bowls, one of sugar cubes, one of lemon wedges. Mara had filled a crystal bowl with fresh fruit and it sat on one of two, slightly stained doilies, the other lying below the vase of roses. In the background played a CD of a Mozart symphony, refined and delicate. Bea and Christy praised everything. "Just right!" and "Pip pip!" they exclaimed in British accents.

Rachel presided over the pouring, and Mara made sure that, no matter what else appealed to them, everyone had a piece of pound cake on her plate.

Constrained by the reality of a tea, the four of them were proper in their gestures and quiet in their speech, but the conversation became truly serious only once: when Bea asked Mara about the drug trial she had begun. Mara described giving herself a practice injection—there was some laughter then—and explained when the study would officially begin and what the doctors had advised her to watch for. At worst, they had said, she could become very sick. At best, she could feel almost immediate improvement. They were hopeful that they were coming close to, perhaps had even found, a cure.

There was silence for a moment. Everyone sharing this tea had lived with the reality of Mara's illness. What would it be like if she were cured? If the walker, the cane, the railings were no longer needed? If the convenient excuse were eliminated?

"You'd have to go to China with me then." Bea announced.

Christy said, "There'd be no getting around ski lessons."

Rachel was quiet, because she suddenly feared being unneeded.

But Mara reached out for her, pulling her close, and said, "Well, now." No one but Mara knew the origin of those words or their significance, but everyone felt comforted.

About the Author

Born in Portland, Oregon, Carol graduated from Willamette University in Salem in 1967 with a degree in English. Three years later she obtained her master's degree from Claremont Graduate School. She taught high school and college English for thirty-one years before retiring from high school administration in 1998. Throughout that time she wrote articles, made conference presentations and wrote a weekly newspaper column called "Grace on Wheels."

Like her mother, Carol was diagnosed with multiple sclerosis. Currently, she is serving as a peer counselor with the Los Angeles chapter of the National MS. Society and sharing her experiences with interested people. She also edits papers sent in response to her tutoring website. Her husband Paul is a successful piano teacher. Carol has two intriguing sons, Eric, 24, and David, 21.